ONE BAD KNIGHT

DEMON KNIGHTS SERIES

HOLLY ROBERDS

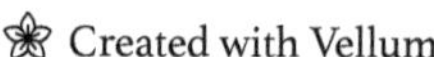 Created with Vellum

BOOKS BY HOLLY ROBERDS

<u>VEGAS IMMORTALS</u>

Death and the Last Vampire

Book 1 - Bitten by Death

Book 2 - Kissed by Death

Book 3 - Seduced by Death

The Beast & the Badass

Book 1 - Breaking the Beast

Book 2 - Claiming the Beast

<u>DEMON KNIGHTS</u>

Book 1 - One Savage Knight

Book 2 - One Bad Knight

<u>LOST GIRLS SERIES</u>

Book 1 - Tasting Red

Book 2 - Chasing Goldie

<u>THE FIVE ORDERS</u>

Book 0.5 – The Knight Watcher

Book 1 - Prophecy Girl

Book 2 - Soulless Son

Book 3 - Tear in the World

Book 4 – Into Darkness

Book 4.5 - Touch of Hell

Book 5 - End Game

* For recommended reading order, visit www.hollyroberds.com

ONE BAD KNIGHT

I'm not the hero.

I'm the bad son they send to do the dirty work when the demons come out.

My brothers save lives, but I ruin them.

I ruined *hers*, years ago.

I should stay away from her.

But something might be coming for the girl I left in pieces all those years ago, and I might not be able to stay away.

The question is what's more dangerous than me?
  And can I for once, not ruin someone?

From the world of The Five Orders, comes a series of standalones tales featuring the Knights of the Light.
  One Bad Knight *can be read as a standalone.*

Dedicated to Rick Astley.
Who knows the words of romance and commitment.
I'll never give YOU up!

1

KAT

Never had I experienced so many sleepless nights. Excitement bubbled in my tummy like pop rocks. I slipped out of bed in the middle of the night because I couldn't sleep again. I would turn eleven in only seven days.

Moonlight filtered in through the French doors, drawing me toward it. I stepped out onto my balcony into the crisp night. Everything was bright from the full moon, so when I looked to the left, the expanse of lawn and gardens stretched out behind the house.

The moon's twin shimmered in the pond out back. Soon, my dad would be throwing parties outside again. His serious, old friends weren't very fun, but I loved how they decorated everything in twinkle lights and brought out the chocolate fountain.

My arms crossed on the railing as I listened to the whisper of palm-sized leaves. A massive sycamore tree shot up past my third-floor balcony and was always active with birds and squirrels, but not a single animal chittered right now.

I'd barely seen my dad the last couple months. Nanny Maureen reminded me this morning, as she braided my hair, that my dad was a very important man and working very hard right now.

He was up for re-election, which meant he was almost never in the house, and when he was, he was in his office and not to be disturbed. I needed to be on my best behavior. If I was a good girl, it would help him focus on what was important.

The wind picked up my hair and whipped it around my face, causing goosebumps from the cold and anticipation to rise along my skin.

But my birthday? The whole day was going to be just my dad and me. None of his campaign people, absolutely no work, and I got to decide what we did the entire day. I chose ice cream and a painting class. I almost picked the museum, but people always bothered him, and I'd end up wandering around the exhibit on my own while people took pictures and asked my dad questions.

But on Saturday we would get messy with paints, and make big, beautiful sunflowers I planned on hanging in my room.

As I inhaled a deep breath of spring night air, I found myself locking eyes with a strange boy sitting in my tree.

I reared back, but the two sharp gray eyes remained fixed on me. A scream froze in my throat.

He seemed about my age, but his eyes held the weight and intensity of someone far older. They pierced me like blades and rooted to the spot.

I scrounged up my voice. "What are you doing up here?" I asked.

He didn't speak, didn't move, just stared at me.

"I'm Kat. What's your name? And how did you get up here?" With a quick look down, I confirmed there wasn't a ladder. I could climb from my balcony into the tree, but the limbs were far too high to get to it from the ground.

Another beat passed before I suppressed the urge to roll my eyes and said, "You aren't a T-Rex. Just because you aren't moving, it doesn't mean I can't see you."

His brows furrowed.

I didn't know how I knew, but I read his expression. "You don't know what a T-Rex is? You know? Like a dinosaur?"

One of his eyebrows dipped as he frowned. I held my hands out to show size. "You know, massive lizards that roamed the earth before humans? Didn't you learn this stuff in school?"

At that, he looked away and his muscles tensed. Suddenly I was afraid he would leave. Strange as it seemed, I didn't want the boy in my tree to leave.

My cheeks grew hot. "I'm sorry, I didn't mean to make you feel bad. I go to a special private school. I don't know what they teach in other schools. That was rude of me." My mom told me when I was little that we were privileged, and I had to be sensitive to that.

He didn't respond, but he didn't leave like I thought he would. The boy continued to stare at me as if trying to figure out all my secrets.

I didn't have many. Only the ones in a shoebox under my bed. It held the diary I kept safe with a small key, the half-empty bottle of my mom's perfume, and one of my dad's special cigars that I told myself I was borrowing. I didn't want to smoke it or anything. I just wanted something grown-up and important in the box.

Something in his intense gaze made me feel... special. Like I was the most interesting thing he'd ever seen in his life. I weirdly felt the same way about the boy with sharp eyes in the tree outside my bedroom window who didn't know about dinosaurs.

A breeze swept through my thin nightgown, and the chill of the bright spring night bit into my me.

Good girls don't let strange boys sit in their trees in the dead of night. And they certainly don't invite them into their house.

What was I doing? I wasn't supposed to talk to strangers. But... kids didn't count. It wasn't dangerous even if the kid was strange.

"Are you cold?" I asked, unable to help myself.

The boy's sandy hair was windblown, and he wore dark clothes under a beat-up jacket. I'd spent my fair share of time hiding in this tree, drawing in my sketchbook so my cousins couldn't bother me. I'd stay up there reading until my fingers turned numb from the cold and it was hard to turn the pages. My dad didn't mind as long as I was at dinner when he told me to be.

The boy didn't answer, but a forward tilt of his head told me everything I needed to know. My mom used to say I was extra good at seeing into people's hearts. Mine told me his was cold.

That bothered me, a lot.

"If you come in, we can make hot chocolate. Since you're taller, I won't have to climb up on the kitchen counter to reach the box." I knew people liked to feel useful.

A thick tree limb stretched over my balcony. I held out a

hand. The boy looked down at my hand and then back at my face, as if calculating something.

I could be patient. I'd once been so patient and still, I'd gotten a squirrel to come over and grab a peanut out of my hand. It took hours, but was so worth it.

Just when I was about to curl my arms around myself to keep what little warmth was left near my body, he moved. The boy easily crept from limb to limb without even having to look. In the last bit of distance between us, he regarded my hand as if still considering leaving.

Then his frozen hand slipped into mine and I closed my fingers around his bigger hand and smiled. For some reason, my heart wanted to burst. This was far better than the squirrel.

I was right. Standing next to him, he was taller than me by almost a head. He smelled like pine, and his face was thin and serious. Most of the boys in my class still had round, ruddy cheeks and obnoxious laughs when they did something stupid or teased each other.

Suddenly, I would have given anything to hear this boy laugh. But I didn't know any jokes, so I just gave him another reassuring smile, and led him inside.

We paused inside my room, as he looked around with a perplexed expression. It felt like bugs were crawling inside my stomach as he examined my special place.

The last time I let someone see my room, it was a girl, Devin, who didn't go to my school, but we met at one of my parents' work parties. She lived in a different town, but I wanted to be friends, so my parents let me have her over for a play date. But after she saw my room, her mouth turned into an "o" and she looked sad. Like I'd done something to hurt her.

I loved my bedroom. Toys, paint sets, and books covered

nearly every inch. The big doll house filled one corner of the room and the other side had a comfy purple chair next to my bookcase. I spent hours there. But the ceiling was my favorite. My mom painted it for me. On the side where my bed was, it looked like a starry night before it morphed into pinks and oranges to a sunny day with fluffy clouds on the other side.

Devin told me I had too many toys and that I was a spoiled brat. I hurriedly offered her my favorite doll to play with to prove I wasn't. She took it, and said she got to play with two more while I could only use one since I had them all the time.

I didn't mind. She came over a few more times, but after a while she only wanted to play with my toys and didn't want to talk to me. The last time I saw her, she grabbed the scissors and started to cut and tear off the heads of some of my stuffed animals. I begged her to stop, but she screamed that I didn't deserve it. Why did I deserve good things, and she didn't? I tried to tell her she deserved good things too, but she didn't listen. My mom found us screaming and sobbing, fluff covering my entire room.

After calling Devin's mom for pickup, my mom tried to console me by saying the girl was very poor and didn't have a lot of toys. That it made her hurt inside and do things to try and fix the hurt, but that Devin's hurt also wasn't my fault. But I knew my room was something to be ashamed of. I loved it, but I never invited anyone over from school. The girls in my class were all interested in makeup and clothes now, but I still liked making up stories and playing by myself.

Suddenly petrified that the boy would tell me I was a spoiled brat and leave, I froze. As if sensing my fear, he turned toward me, his face softening for the first time. It wasn't a smile, more thoughtful and almost... protective. Then he stepped in closer to me and I knew he was telling me he wasn't going to leave.

I swallowed the lump in my throat and led him out to the hallway. I didn't turn on the lights, so we crept in the dark, down the big winding staircase, past the sitting room, library, and my dad's office until we got to the kitchen at the back of the house.

With the boy's help, we got down some hot chocolate packets. I was careful to boil water but not let the kettle scream and wake anyone up. Though I tried to get the boy to sit, he refused. He just stood at the edge of the big island, casting glances at the door as if someone might come in any moment.

I dumped extra marshmallows into his and slid the mug toward him with a smile. He looked at me, then back at the mug. Leaning over, he sniffed at it. I tried to suppress my giggle, not wanting him to feel weird, but it came out anyway. He shot me an uncertain look before his lips gave me a lopsided imitation of a return smile. My heart fluttered in response.

He bent over, his nose dipping in the whipped cream. Then he jerked up. Though he looked silly with white fluff on his face, his eyes turned sharp and focused. Steps approached down the hall.

My dad entered the kitchen, still wearing his work clothes, which were rumpled. Though it was past midnight, he'd just gotten home from work. My head snapped back to the boy, but he was gone. He'd disappeared, like magic.

"Kat. What are you doing up late?" my dad asked with a frown. I was about to explain when he caught sight of the second mug. "Is that for me?"

Deep lines creased under his tired eyes, and his thick

hair was messy. His usually pale skin neared orange because one of his advisors told him a spray tan would look better on TV. But it made his skin smell weird.

I heard tense whispers in the hallways of our house for weeks that the election wasn't going well.

I nodded mutely, looking back at the spot where my new friend disappeared. The boy didn't want to be seen. He'd been scared. And I worried if I told anyone about him, he'd be mad I didn't keep his secret. So I said, "Yes, Daddy. You can have the one with extra marshmallows."

"Thanks sweetie," he said, then he paused. "You look more like your mother every day."

My dad and I looked almost nothing alike, but we had the same upturned eye shape and thin nose. My medium brown skin, dark hair, and full lips made me look more my mom.

I smiled at first, but then I let it slide off my face. My dad hadn't looked up from the marshmallows as he said it. Something about the way he said it made me feel he didn't like that I resembled my mother. He seemed... unhappy. My fingers picked at my nightgown. Maybe if I were like the other girls and put makeup on, it would make me look different from my mom. Would he want that?

Then my dad picked up the mug, ruffled my hair, and made me promise to go back to bed once I finished my hot chocolate.

When he left, I sighed and my shoulders relaxed. I didn't realize they'd gotten all scrunched up. Then I raced to the kitchen door leading to the outside. No sign of the boy. He wasn't in the tree, either.

I couldn't fit the boy in the shoebox under my bed, but he was my biggest and best secret.

....

THE NEXT NIGHT, he was there again. Waiting, watching from the tree. It took less convincing to get him to join me this time. I got him to try hot chocolate finally, and he immediately wanted three more cups. By the third one he looked positively green in the face, and I had to keep my giggles quiet.

It went on that way the entire week. I'd wake up in the middle of the night, too excited for both my birthday and my new secret friend. Every night, I'd find him there in the tree and he'd leave before dawn.

I showed him all my toys, but he seemed particularly drawn to the picture of me and my parents by my bed. I picked it up and kissed it, explaining my mom died four years ago and I missed her so much it hurt. But she was an angel in heaven now. From his serious expression, I guessed his mommy was in heaven too, though I didn't know for sure.

Another night I took him into the living room to show him our new kittens. While petting one of the little tabbies, I explained we had to give them all away but weren't they cute?

He regarded the small fluff balls with a serious expression. When I handed him a kitten, panic crossed his face.

"You'll be okay. Just pet them gently, like this." I took his hand and showed him how.

"What do you use them for?" he asked. It was the first time I heard him speak. My stomach somersaulted, and I instantly wanted to hear his voice again.

"Use them for?" I asked. Wasn't it obvious? "You love them."

Something I said must have upset him because his face closed off from me. He bent over the kitten he held and continued to pet it the way I showed him.

I leaned in and dropped a kiss on the kitten's head. It let out a tiny mewl.

Mimicking me, the boy kissed the kitten's head and it mewled again. I got another one of those lopsided, "almost" smiles. My heart fluttered again. We took turns leaning over and kissing the kitten's head, until our faces bumped into each other.

Rubbing my forehead, I laughed too loud. I clapped my hand over my mouth and his eyes followed the movement. When I eventually dropped my hand, he continued to stare. Then he leaned forward and pressed his lips against mine.

My heart nearly jumped out of my chest. It was quick and warm. I'd seen people kiss on TV, but it felt different from what I thought it would. It was squishier. But I liked it. I couldn't stop grinning at him, and he gave me an even more lopsided smile. In the morning, I wrote three whole pages in my diary about it. It had been the best week ever.

THE NIGHT before my birthday I practically sprung out of bed. I made the boy promise to come back at midnight when it was officially my birthday. We could celebrate together. I was going to show him my secret shoebox. Maybe even let him read a couple pages out of my diary if he wanted, but I would choose which ones.

I tied on my pink robe and tried to do everything I could to distract myself, but time moved impossibly slow. Not even my sketchbook could hold my attention, so I went around the room, rearranging my toys.

Five minutes before midnight, I heard something boom. The sound had come from all the way downstairs.

Maybe my dad had come home. He hadn't been home most nights, making it easier to sneak around with my big secret.

I didn't bother being quiet as I went down the stairs. Another crash, and I broke into a run, wanting to catch what was happening. Light spilled out from under my dad's office doors, so I pushed them open.

I froze, eyes widening as I tried to take everything in. Papers and books were strewn everywhere. Broken statues from the shelves were scattered on the throw rug. The double doors leading to the back terrace were wide open, the sheer curtains flapping almost violently as the breeze swept through.

My father lay slumped over his desk and the boy stood next to him, covered in my father's blood.

No. No, this wasn't right. Everything was all wrong.

There was so much blood.

My father wasn't moving. He should be moving. I didn't like how still he was.

The curtains slapped against the doors even harder and a dark, monstrous shadow swelled from them. It floated into the office.

My skin turned to ice, and I couldn't take a breath.

The dark mass twisted and turned over my father, as if inspecting him. The boy turned to look at the darkness, his lips thin and eyes hard. He wasn't afraid.

But I was terrified. I clutched my robe, feet glued to the floor, afraid if I moved, the darkness would notice me.

A strange half groan escaped my throat despite myself. I

grabbed my own neck, but it was too late. The shadow jerked up. My heart pounded against my ribs. It saw me. It started toward me, and a scream got caught in my throat. I still couldn't force myself to move.

Part of me prayed I would wake up from this nightmare.

The boy stepped in between us and lifted a hand up at the monstrous being. Light shot out of his hand as he said some strange words I didn't recognize.

With a screech the shadow twisted up into the air and blew back out the doors, like a furious tornado.

I was left shaking like a leaf, still clutching at my robe. The boy turned around to face me. He set his hands on my shoulders as if he wanted to help but didn't know how.

The boy wore a pained expression as he looked back at me. Was it regret or pity I saw in his eyes?

I desperately wanted him to say something. Anything. The pressure in my chest felt like it would explode at any second as warm drops hit my face. I was crying. I tried to look past the boy to where my dad lay, still unmoving.

The boy put a hand on my face to guide me to look back at him instead. He searched my eyes and visibly swallowed. Then he lifted his hand and gently swept his palm down my forehead until it forced me to close my eyes.

I continued to shake, but he removed his hands from my shoulder and eyes. A tear slid onto my lips. Then I felt the soft pressure of his mouth on mine for the second time. The saltiness of my tears mingled with the kiss.

Then the air around me turned cold. I opened my eyes. The boy was gone.

The grandfather clock in the hall struck midnight, announcing my eleventh birthday and the death of my father.

2

GATSBY

Twelve years later.

Gonna pretend you don't feel that? a voice whispered from the back of my mind.

Even the roar of my motorcycle cruising down the highway couldn't drown out the feeling. The best way I could describe it was a dark heat. Though I neared eighty-five miles per hour, the intensity left a metallic, sour taste in my mouth.

As much as I tried to ignore it, it continued to tug at me with tiny, hateful claws.

Something from the hell dimension was near, and something very bad was about to happen.

It's not your problem anymore, Gatsby. Don't get involved.

Under my helmet, I sneered, unable to ignore its call, pulling off the highway. For ten minutes, I followed the feeling until I found myself slowing in a suburban neighborhood.

My heavy boots hit the pristine pavement of a sidewalk lined with little spring flowers.

A man like me didn't belong here. Not in this cute little cul-de-sac where civilians lived their normal little lives, went to work, and then came home and ate dinner together as a family.

A man like me belonged in the hell I'd been trained to fight my entire life. If anyone peeked out their lace curtains to see a tattooed man with his black motorcycle and pure hate in his eyes, they'd likely call the cops.

But the cops couldn't help them. A Knight of the Light could. A warrior, trained in secret to fight the demons from the Stygian, a hell dimension that had been bleeding into ours for centuries.

But I wasn't a Knight of the Light. Not anymore. Not that I had truly ever been one of them. But their pristine, light-wielding hands weren't here, and I was.

The dark fire tugged me harder, drawing my attention to the blue house with a bird bath out front and a yard sign announcing there was an honor roll student in the house.

The crickets chirped obnoxiously, filling the night air, as I stood in front of the white door.

You can still walk away. You can get back on the motorcycle and not make this your problem.

Knowing how these small neighborhoods were, I grasped the handle. It turned over without resistance, and I walked right into the living room. The TV blared bright colors of a cartoon as a strange group of figures and a talking dog ran from room to room, chased by a ghost. Lamps filled the house with cozy, warm light, and a burning candle filled the room with the overpowering scent of peonies.

My boots fell silently on the rose-colored carpet as I went farther into the house. The kitchen sink was filled with dirty plates, and the scent of roast chicken still lingered in the air.

As I ascended the stairs, that hot buzz persisted, and I caught a whiff of sulfur. Evidence of the demonic presence.

Down one end of the hall, a door stood open to an empty master bedroom with an absurd number of decorative pillows on the bed. On the other end of the hall, there were two rooms caddy-corner to each other. One was open —a little boy's room, covered in spaceships and dinosaurs, while the closed door had a big sign with pink, curvy letters announcing it was "Cecilia's Room" and to keep out.

I unsheathed my sword from my back before my boot slammed into the door. It crashed open. My eyes instantly watered while the carpet squished noisily under my boots. The room reeked of gasoline, burning my nose and throat. A young boy and an older girl with matching brown eyes and the same straight blond hair sat tied up on the bed. Clean white socks had been shoved into their mouths; their red-rimmed eyes overflowed with tears.

Someone had used white spray paint on the rose carpet to make a pentagram with several glyphs. The children were about to be sacrificed.

As soon as they saw me, the two children screamed through their makeshift gags.

Something struck me on my back, sending me staggering a few steps as the pain cut through my ability to breathe.

My hand caught her wrist before the next blow. I turned to face the children's mother, who wore yoga pants and an oversized tee that declared it was Wine O'clock Somewhere. Dyed red hair was cropped in a short, sharp haircut, and she held the weight of a woman who put everyone else's needs before her own.

With a twist of her wrist, I forced her to release the little league bat.

Her words came out as the inhuman hiss of a demon. "Yous will die. In the name of Azgexin."

I twisted the possessed woman's arm further, forcing her onto her knees.

"Get out of this woman," I demanded.

Lips stretched up on either side of the woman's face, far past what should have been possible, nearly reaching her ears. It made for a bone-chilling grin. "You knows I can't. Once wes are ins, we can'ts get outs. And I likes this one."

It was true. Once a demon possessed a person, it couldn't leave the vessel on its own.

Recognition sparked on her face. "We knows you. Dark son of the Light. If you wants me out, you have to send me back."

My spine stiffened. The glittering in the woman's dark eyes told me the demon knew far too much about me.

"You can't gets me outs, can you? We all knows you aren't like the others. You cannots use your power. You are the broken boy, the bad one, the dark one."

I twisted her arm harder, earning me a pained grunt from the demon inside. Muffled cries rose from behind me.

To the children, I was still hurting their mother—even if she had been about to sacrifice them to the demon overlord Azgexin.

My fingers tightened on my sword as my teeth ground together.

The demon was right. My power had never been strong enough to exorcise the dark spirits back to the Stygian. Not to mention when I could harness my magic, it was shaky at best, working in short, unreliable bursts. If I were one of my brothers, they would have been able to do it. Jettison this fucker out of this woman's body and send it back to the hell dimension it came from.

But they weren't here. I was.

"Release the woman," I demanded again with a snarl. "Or I'll chop her head off and suck your disgusting fucking essence into a vacuum cleaner where you can spend eternity trapped in a bag of broken Cheerios and cat hair." That wasn't exactly possible, but demons weren't the smartest. It also couldn't know I was bluffing.

The mother was trapped in the demon's hold. If I killed her, the demonic spirit would only spiral out and find another host. The woman would be dead, while the demon went free. It's what made these spirits one of the nastiest to deal with.

"I'll kills you and I'm taking those two withs me." The hate-filled eyes pinned the children behind me, that terrifying grin still in place.

"You won't kill anyone," I promised. "We are going downstairs, and someone else is going to come handle you." I knew who to call. I'd tie her up in the kitchen or living room. And then one of my brothers would show up and do what I couldn't. And I'd be long gone before they got to the house.

The woman narrowed her eyes. "Nos, I have a better idea," it rasped in delight.

Red pin pricks ignited in her eyes. Her skin turned almost unbearably hot under my grip.

Fuck.

The demon was going to burn through the woman from the inside out, setting her ablaze. With the carpet soaked in gasoline. If the demon caused the woman to combust into flames, the entire room would ignite like a powder keg. I wouldn't have time to get myself out, much less the kids.

My teeth clenched so hard, I was sure they would crack. I thrust my sword through the heart of the woman though it felt like I was running myself through.

Instantly, the red lights in her eyes were extinguished, and her body sagged.

The screams behind me turned frantic. The two kids had just watched me murder their mother in front of their eyes.

The woman's mouth slowly shrank back down to its normal size. Black mist spewed from her mouth like vomit before shooting up through the roof and disappearing. The demon got away.

Brown eyes blinked at me, tears filling them, as blood dribbled out the corner of the woman's mouth.

"My babies," she rasped. And then she was gone.

The crying and screams behind me only increased in intensity.

Darkness swallowed my heart and chewed on it with a thousand fangs.

This is what you are for, Gatsby. You bring death and destruction.

Blue and red lights swam in through the bedroom window. Someone had seen me arrive after all. They likely saw me let myself into the house and called the cops.

I gently laid the woman down and stood. I couldn't bring myself to meet the eyes of her children. So, I left them there, tied up and gagged, with their dead mother's body on the floor.

Disgust coated my throat.

Someone else, someone better, would help them.

I didn't help. I destroyed.

Slipping out the back, I thought of how I'd have to steal another motorcycle now. It was too far to walk back to her house, and bikes made it easy to slip in and out of places without people noticing or being able to follow.

And if I'd make sure of one thing, it was that I remained alone, and under the radar. I'd lived my entire life enslaved to a cause that wasn't my own. I wouldn't give up my freedom or independence for anyone. Not ever again.

Even if I deserved to burn in hell for what I'd just done here.

And I'd no doubt, hell would catch up to me sooner or later.

3

KAT

"Give me two minutes," I said, scratching Bear's ears. My dog's nails tapped across the floor, sticking to my side, though he knew he wasn't allowed in certain parts of the house. My massive chocolate brown Newfoundland had earned his namesake on sight. He might be nearly as big as a bear, but he was as cuddly as an oversized teddy.

Bear paused at the doorway, knowing he wasn't allowed in the dining room when there was food. I gave him a scratch behind the ears before he trotted off in search of his own kibble.

"I'm afraid I have to skip breakfast this morning," I said even as I strode into the dining room.

My uncle and two cousins were seated at one end of the long table. They never failed to be dressed in their suits by 7:00 a.m. Gabe didn't bother to look up from his tablet, no doubt reading the *Wall Street Journal*. His older brother Dave was on a call with someone and using his stern "business" voice.

Hot coffee, scrambled eggs, bacon and fresh croissants were laid out across the white table cloth. The current chef had made plenty more, and it sat in covered dishes on a credenza off to the side. But I just grabbed an apple from the wire cage of fruit. I had a fire in me right now, and I needed to get it on canvas before I lost it.

"Katherine, we need to talk," my Uncle John said, pointing at the seat next to Gabe. "You've put it off enough, and the painting can wait."

I rolled the apple in my hand, trying to think of an excuse to avoid the talk, but he pinned me with a look that said there was no getting out of it this time.

I dropped into the seat next to Gabe and set down my bag. Since I was staying, I reached over and poured myself some French press from the silver coffee pot.

"I feel like you spend more time at that little studio than at home these days," my uncle said, trying to not let his judgement filter in through his words and failing miserably.

I smoothed a hand over my hair. I hadn't stopped to shower after waking up in a mood I couldn't describe, but wanted to discover in color. My looks didn't just contrast my family's, they completely clashed with them.

I'd thrown on my ripped jeans and my favorite band tee, both already covered in paint splatters. I'd pulled my dark brown hair up into a messy bun, and hadn't even bothered to wash my face. Funny how I was the only thing that looked out of place in this room, considering it was my house. My uncle and cousins had moved in after my dad died, but they fit the traditional aesthetic far better than me.

Like my father, they were dark-haired with pale skin and red undertones. My mother was a mix of African, white, and East Indian heritage, with coffee-colored skin, while mine was a lighter, golden brown.

My uncle's supporters always rushed to tell me how exotic my looks were, as if they were trying to show how cool they were. But I was born and raised in Denver, Colorado, and the most exotic thing about me was my taste in cuisine because I'd try almost anything from anywhere.

Realizing my uncle and I were going to have a conversation, Dave got up and excused himself to the next room to continue his call.

My uncle rested his elbows on the table to interlace his fingers. Gray crept in at his temples and was fast traveling upward, but he wouldn't let me dye it. I noticed, not for the first time, the wide bridge of his nose. I'd tried to draw it many times, but I always got the bump wrong.

"We need to talk about your birthday, Katherine."

A sinking sensation slid down my stomach. I sipped on my favorite roast, but it only added acid to the unsettling mix in my tummy.

"It's your twenty-third birthday, and I think it's appropriate we mark the occasion appropriately."

"A party," Gabe said next to me, not looking up from the article he was reading. "Dad is talking about a party."

My gut churned harder. "Don't we already have a party or gala every single night this week for your campaign?" This week was already going to be insanely busy. Even just thinking about how much pointless, overly polite small talk was in my future made me want to crawl back into bed.

And I didn't want another party, not even for myself.

Every year on my birthday, I did my best to keep my head down and get through to the next day as fast as possible. If anyone found out and got me a cake or a present, I had to paint on a smile, and pretend I enjoyed the attention and celebration.

While I wasn't thrilled about the barrage of events this week, at least they weren't focused on me.

"Yes, but a party celebrating your future plans would not only help me, it would be a great marker for your future," my uncle said, watching me carefully.

"With my luck, it would be a disaster," I said with a nervous laugh, pushing my cup away. "Every time I get on my phone, I see videos of big parties being stomped out by some hell demon or swarmed by evil ghosts."

Over a year ago, a hell mouth opened in the mountains, releasing all kinds of demonic creatures and evil spirits.

It didn't seem real at first, especially not in our gated neighborhood where security walked the streets and kept things locked down. But I'll never forget the day I was driving in another town to shop for brushes and watched a mass of mottled black demons fly by, causing the people in the streets to run into a panic. One grabbed a woman right off the streets in front of me. I'll never forget the look of terror in her eyes.

I abandoned my trip for art supplies and my hands hadn't stopped shaking for two days.

Like everyone else, I'd wondered if the world was ending.

But life went on. It always went on. However unjust or unlikely, it did.

Uncle John interrupted my disturbing memory. "All the more reason why we should try to promote a sense of cele-bration and joy around this time."

"You know you are going to win this election, right, Uncle John?" I asked with a cheeky grin.

"Indeed," he said, wiping the corner of his mouth with his napkin. "This week there will be several events for our more financially supportive voters to come meet and mingle. Can I count on you to show up and support?"

I hated when he used his politician's voice on me, but I nodded as I sipped more of the French press. This was important to him. And if my dad were alive, it would be him running for re-election right now, no doubt. I owed it to my father and to my uncle to be there.

"He wants you to go with Jimi," Gabe interrupted again without looking up.

My uncle shot my cousin a sharp glance, then it softened as he looked at me. "I know you two are enjoying a casual spring fling, but it would speak well to the press to have two such politically powerful families aligned." My cheeks flushed, but he went on before I could respond. "And then there is the matter of our agreement."

My stomach dropped, and I picked up the apple again, tossing it back and forth between my hands.

"You know I'm very proud of you for getting your economics degree," he said.

I kept my face carefully blank. I'd done it, but I hated every minute of it. If I hadn't been able to take every artistic elective I could to balance out the drudgery, I wouldn't have made it. I tossed the apple faster.

He went on. "And I gave you the last several months off to play artist, but it's time to start submitting to the law programs like we agreed." My uncle reached out and covered my hands, stilling my movements. "I really think you'd enjoy Harvard. The East Coast has some of the best country clubs, and you have a lot of friends out there."

A lot of *his* friends lived out there, but I didn't bother to correct him. I knew he only wanted the best for me.

"Your parents would want this," he added in a low voice, twisting the invisible knife that never left my gut.

"My gallery show is in two days. Do you think you'll come?" I asked, changing the subject entirely.

My uncle released my hands and leaned back in his seat with a sigh, knowing I was desperately trying to worm my way out of this. "Send the information to my assistant, and I'll make sure she arranges it."

I'd already sent it to everyone twice, but I'd do it again.

Dave chose that moment to come back in and sit down, now done with his phone call.

"I'd love if my whole family showed up to the show," I said, addressing my cousins too.

They exchanged a quick glance.

"Come on," I said, sticking an elbow into Gabe's ribs. "It's my first show ever."

"We are a family," my uncle said, a warning lacing his tone.

"Sure," Gabe mumbled.

"Yeah," Dave agreed, though he looked like he'd rather give up his favorite golf club and switch to generic hair gel than come to my event.

I let out a breath I didn't know I'd been holding in. "Great. I'll RSVP for you guys so you are already on the gallery's guest list. And..." I slid out of my chair, picking up my bag while still gripping the apple tightly. "I'll start on those applications for law school tonight."

Fair was fair. Though the idea of living on the East Coast, far from my family, and studying law was a future painted in dull, lifeless grays.

A smile spread across my uncle's face. "Excellent,

Katherine. And of course, at your birthday party, I can introduce you to some friends who attended Harvard Law."

"I never agreed to a party for me," I shot over my shoulder as I walked out.

I'd been about to head out the door, when I realized I had forgotten my keys. I turned and raced back up the staircases to my bedroom.

It had drastically changed over the years, as I replaced toys with pieces of art that sang to my soul, usually strange pieces I'd find at flea markets, from artists on Instagram, or from sweet old men who spent their lives in Italy, painting the scenery.

But the one thing that never changed was the ceiling mural my mother had painted. I kissed my fingers and sent the kiss upward to the ceiling. "Hi mom," I whispered out of habit.

Spotting my keys on the desk, I went to grab them. With the cool metal in my hand, I should have left, but I paused and looked out the French doors leading to my balcony. My gaze lingered on the massive tree outside. Big leaves already filled out the branches. My heart sped up as I started to get that familiar sensation.

I tried to tell myself it was my imagination. No one was watching me. When I looked outside, I sternly told myself there would be no presence of familiar serious, sharp eyes.

The fear and anticipation that the boy would come back always intensified in the days leading up to my birthday, but this year it was worse than ever.

Especially since the presence of demons had become public knowledge in the last year.

When I tried to tell people what happened that night, they said I was traumatized by finding my father murdered. I'd been told repeatedly it was emotional stress that had caused me to see such scary visions and imagine a boy who never showed up on the security cameras though I swore he'd been with me all week long. My uncle was unreachable at the time, so Child Protective Services decided I needed to be institutionalized. I'd been lumped in with kids who were self-harming, on drugs, from abusive homes. I just needed someone to listen to me, and no one would. I was so grateful when my uncle rescued me from that place, I never spoke of it again.

I shuddered, recalling those three weeks in a white room, drooling from the drugs, trapped with the nightmares in my mind. But now...

In the last year, I barely slept, thinking of that dark shadow in my father's office. Demons were real. I'd seen video footage of monsters on the news and social media. Even though I saw the same reports every day of some horrible creature crashing a park, or leaving behind the barest trace of their victims.

But that night had been so long ago, I still wondered if maybe I had made it up. All those years ago, I'd felt like Wendy from the fairytale *Peter Pan*. Had the boy in the tree outside my bedroom asked me to follow him to Neverland, I wouldn't have hesitated to put my hand in his and go wherever he wanted. But he'd left without me. Flown far away, leaving me to deal with blood, death, and nightmares all on my own.

I must have made him up. No real person could be so cruel.

My hand curled around the keys until the sharp edges bit into my fingers. I swore I could almost feel *his* presence brushing against my skin, he felt so close. Heat crawled under my skin as the inevitable question popped up.

Would I want to see him again? The boy who may have

murdered my father? The one who left me to deal with the fallout of what was the worst night of my life?

I turned and stomped out of the room. I was being ridiculous. He never came back, and he never would. Even if he hadn't killed my father, he'd still left me there, all alone.

I needed to focus on what was important and real. My uncle's election, and my future in law.

Love was duty, and I would show my family I loved them more than anything by doing my due diligence.

No matter how the prospect made me feel like a cage was closing in around me.

4

GATSBY

You can give it one more day, I convinced myself once again. *You can stay just one more day to make sure she's alright.*

I dropped out of the tree into the yard after Kat had gone, keys in hand. For a moment she'd stared right at me, where I crouched in the sycamore. I was certain she'd seen me as a myriad of emotions, from fear, to anger, to longing, crossed her face.

But then she'd turned and left. I wasn't sure if I was relieved or disappointed. She hadn't seen me in twelve years, but I had seen her.

Three times since that night in her father's study, to be exact.

Twice, I hadn't even realized where I was going until I sat right outside her bedroom in that familiar tree. The first time, she'd been fourteen, scribbling over a thick textbook while I sat perfectly still, mesmerized for hours. The second time she was eighteen, and blasting music in her room as she danced around with her dog and sang off-key.

And now I was back again, and here I stayed, for almost two weeks.

Even in the gray morning light, I easily evaded the cameras on the property, scaling the fence back to where I'd parked my motorcycle.

As I secured my helmet, the roar of another motorcycle came from nearby. Katherine was on her way to the studio. Her schedule wasn't hard to figure out. Her routine rarely varied. I knew she tried to get to the studio first thing and would occasionally visit with the other artists in the coffee shop situated below the studio. Two days a week she taught art classes to children in the afternoon. Four times a week, she went to Krav Maga classes, kicking, punching, and grappling until she was soaked in sweat. The evenings were about supporting her uncle's campaign, and spending time with family. She always showed up at dinner on time to entertain her uncle's frequent guests, or fold pamphlets for one of his events.

In the past two weeks, I'd learned how little she slept. How in the dead of night, Kat would sneak out to the studio. While everyone else slept, she painted furiously in the empty room, dark circles heavy under her eyes until she could get whatever plagued her onto canvas.

But wherever she went, I'd be right there, watching. Watching each stroke of paint, the way her tongue stuck out of her mouth and the line that formed between her eyes when she observed her work, displeased with something about it. From the empty building balcony next to the studio, I'd watch how her eyes almost became glazed when she got in the zone, brushing madly yet so intentionally.

My fingers paused on the ignition.

"What are you doing, Gatsby?" I hissed to myself. "You shouldn't be here. You already ruined her life."

I should go. I didn't get involved. When I did, it only ended in death and destruction.

The faces of two crying children haunted me. That had been weeks ago, but I still saw them whenever I closed my eyes.

My brothers were heroes. If I stayed, I was going to make things worse.

Even as I decided Kat was better off without me, I started up my bike and headed in the familiar direction of her studio.

One last time. This would be the last day I watched.

Tonight, I'd get on my bike and drive out of town without looking back.

5

——————

KAT

"Up here," Viet pointed at the top corner of my half-done painting, "I love the play of light and dark. It's like they are battling for dominance, and I'm not sure which one will win."

I tried to cover up my smile, but I loved how she instantly got what I was trying to do.

"You are beyond talented, Kat," Viet said as she nudged my shoulder. She was practically half my height, but twice as talented. Her hair was fuchsia this week, and she made her eyes more cat-like with winged eyeliner. She'd cut up a shirt that said "The Future is Female," so it showed off her generous, plus-sized breasts. The ripped jeans that accentuated her generous, curvy rear looked as though they lost a cage match with a wolverine.

Viet preferred to sculpt clay, and gray bits dotted her clothes and stained her hands. I adored her work and had already bought several busts colored in bright neon splotches that instantly energized me when I set eyes on them. But where in my secret heart of hearts I wanted to be a professional artist, Viet did it for fun, selling a couple sculptures online from time to time.

We'd met eight months ago when I first started painting at the studio. She continually made a point to come over to chat with me despite my polite but cool demeanor. I wasn't looking for friends, and in my experience, people got weird, angry or tried to cozy up to me once they found out who my uncle was. But Viet wore me down with invites of pizza and wine and our mutual love for Jane Austen had sealed the deal.

I couldn't help the smile curving my lips. "You think?" That earned me another nudge.

"Don't pretend you don't know you're talented." Viet rolled her eyes though she still grinned. "Your portraits are powerful, and this gallery show is going to explode your name as an artist!"

My feelings instantly went to war. To be able to paint for a living would be my dream, but being there for my family was more important. There was a certain image I needed to maintain for their sake.

In a gentler voice, Viet added, "And I bet you'd for sure go mega famous if you pulled out whatever you have in that closet over there."

I followed her gaze to the locked closet at the back corner of the studio. Only Sam, the studio owner, and I had a key. When I first started painting here, I made a deal with Sam to rent the storage space.

While having the code to the front door meant any of us residents could paint or sculpt when the mood struck us, I was there more than anyone. Countless times I found myself painting alone at 2:00 a.m., unable to sleep until I put the image down that burned its way into my brain onto canvas. It was those paintings I locked away into my private closet collection.

"Not gonna happen," I said, nudging Viet back.

She stomped a foot in frustration. "You are such a tease. You should let your best girl see them at least."

I worked to cover up my smile.

"Are we still going out tonight?" I asked, changing the subject.

Viet's face brightened. "Absolutely! I've got this new little black number that I'm going to pour myself into and then dance my butt off in."

"Perfect," I said. "Though I think your butt is what brings all the boys to the yard." Then I pinched her plus-sized rear, earning a squeal and a swat. She winked at me, knowing all too well how true that was.

Her smile faltered. "Are you going to invite Jimi?"

I'd been casually dating Jimi for the last two months. Our families were old friends, and he was also deeply entrenched in the political lifestyle. But between my painting schedule and his polo games and golfing, we usually only saw each other at fundraiser dinners, or rallies to support my uncle. But this week, there was a party every single night, and I knew he'd be at all of them.

Viet had carefully emptied her expression, but I knew she wasn't a big fan of Jimi or his 'goon squad' as she called them. Alan and Ross almost always seemed attached to his hip.

I shrugged my shoulder. "It's casual, and he's probably got something going already."

"Can I ask?" she said in a conspiratorial whisper. "When you guys make out or do the deed, does he ever stop flashing that perfect, pasted-on smile?"

I snorted. "Yes, believe it or not, he's not always camera-ready, Viet."

Jimi was classically handsome to be sure, often mistaken for a Kennedy. And I really appreciated having a buddy for the seemingly endless events. He could small talk for hours without breaking a sweat. Which meant I could stand silently by his side and let him do all the heavy lifting with people I had almost nothing in common with.

But romantically, Jimi's appeal had waned after a few make-out sessions. I didn't mention to Viet that he tended to moan like he was eating the most scrumptious meal when we kissed. He made me feel like a bowl of excellent soup.

Viet lifted her arms and swayed her hips as if she were in the club already. "Our usual place?"

"Is there any other place that will let me stash my motor-cycle gear behind the bar *and* give us free drinks?"

Viet shook her head with a giggle. "They aren't free when you tip the way you do."

I blew a raspberry at her and pushed her away so I could finish up. Tonight, I'd drink and dance away any thoughts of Harvard Law, my birthday, or the anniversary of my dad's death.

~

THE LIGHTS STROBED in shades of blue, and my skin felt electric from the crisp citrus of the gin and tonic I downed when we'd first gotten here. The music pulsated up into my body and I felt free.

Here, no one could tell me what to do. No one knew who I was, and no one would frown at the cheap beer I drank, or the way I danced. I reveled in the simplicity of wearing a revealing halter dress without the censure of my family or our acquaintances. The midnight blue fabric sparkled and plunged at the neckline almost to my belly button, while the hem rode a dangerous line at the bottom of my thighs. Here, I wasn't Katherine, niece of Senator John Hart. Here I was just Kat.

A guy wearing a designer tee with a smile that shone even in the darkness of the club approached me. I wasn't sure I wanted to dance with anyone other than myself, but he followed all the rules. Making deliberate eye contact, he shot me a sultry smile. He was cute enough, so I held eye contact, giving the nonverbal cue that he could approach me. Soon, he sidled up next to me. Our rhythm was off, but he made up for it by occasionally spinning me, making me laugh.

Something in my chest unclenched. This was freedom. I didn't have to think about being perfect here, and I savored these precious few days I had left. There was no question I'd get into Harvard. In New England, I'd be under such intense pressure and scrutiny, there would be no days or nights like this. Especially when my uncle's inevitable re-election win came about. All the right people would mob around me, like the first time he'd been elected.

Through the strobing lights, a pair of eyes caught my attention at the edge of the dance floor.

The hairs on the back of my neck rose. Those eyes were focused on me with unerring intensity.

As I danced and the lights pulsated in different colors, I couldn't see who they belonged to. But they pierced me. Made me feel exposed in the middle of a crowd.

Then the lights settled, and the beat dropped, both pieces of sensory overload falling away like gauzy curtains drifting to the floor. A face came into view. My breath caught in my chest.

The man had a hard, dangerous look that hit me like a physical blow. From his hard, square jaw covered in unruly stubble, to the way he stared at me through the sandy hair that fell in his eyes. He wore a black shirt that clung to his muscled chest. Black ink crawled up his neck and down his exposed arms in elaborate tattooed designs. Everything about him screamed trouble with a capital T.

Suddenly it was hard to swallow. Hard to breathe. His eyes pierced through me, as though he could see everything inside of me—all the dark and light bits struggling in the daily chaos of life. The floor all but disappeared under me, but I was grounded in those eyes as if they were my only gravity.

My hand itched to slash blacks and blues across a canvas until his broad, foreboding form emerged from the darkness. I'd never been so struck by the need to paint before. I was overwhelmed by the strong sense that I would die if I didn't get hold of a paintbrush soon.

My dancing lost its luster. In an attempt to brush off the man's attention, I went back to swaying my hips and focused on my dance partner. As my dance partner drew near, the foot of distance closed to mere inches. The scent of his strong cologne mixed with that of cheap beer.

Without even looking, I could feel the man across the

room move. Slowly, steadily, he weaved his way through the crowd. My skin prickled under his unerring gaze, and I felt as though a predator was stalking me.

My partner's hands fell to rest on my hips. I couldn't help but feel a flash of anxiety zip along my skin. I got the strange sense I'd done something wrong with this other man watching, but I shook it off.

This was where I came to be free. I refused to be intimidated by the judgement of some rando with a face carved by renegade angels. I attempted to lose myself to the dance again, intending to reclaim my buzz.

My dance partner's movements stalled, and his half-lidded eyes widened. Shooting an apologetic, and slightly fearful, smile, he mumbled something I couldn't hear before turning and heading back in the direction of the bar.

Prickles of danger raced up my spine, as I sensed the presence of someone taller and broader coming up from behind. I shivered. When I tried to turn toward him, strong hands grabbed my hips, keeping me facing forward.

He immediately set me into a rhythm that was half time to the music. Time slowed down, as a muscled wall met my bare back. I could feel the ridges of his warm pectorals, and the contact felt pornographic for such a public place.

Whereas my previous partner made eye contact, getting nonverbal consent to dance with me, this guy had come up from behind and encroached on my space. No matter how titillating I found this man, I had standards. I jerked away, ready to head to the other side of the bar and away from the dangerous entity at my back. But his fingers dug into my hips, pulling me back against him again. He didn't want me facing him or walking away.

The combination of the rough movement and the intoxicating scent of sex pheromones and virile man rolled over me. Despite myself, my knees turned to jelly and liquid heat gathered at my center. Visions of what else his rough hands could do ran through my imagination.

I was so used to being treated like a porcelain doll; I almost welcomed his brazen moves. But I still didn't submit to anyone, no matter how hot.

I tilted my head to the side, so he could hear me when I shouted. "You chased my date away."

I could only catch the wicked curve of his lips, and another ripple raced down my spine, informing my brain how screwed I was. Because a lower portion of my body was now in charge.

The man aligned his mouth to the side of my head, so he didn't have to shout. His hot breath fanned against my ear and my nipples instantly tightened. "You were dancing with me before I came over."

"Who says I want to dance with you?" Even as I said the words, an achy heat spread between my legs, and I squeezed them together as if I could keep the sudden wetness at bay. The bass of the music traveled up my feet, past my legs, penetrating my lower belly, only making it worse.

"Who says we ever stopped?" His voice rumbled through the column of my neck.

Before I could make sense of his response, his hardness ground against my ass. My mouth went dry. With an instinctual shift in my hips, I directed him to rub along the sensitive seam of my rear.

I might have needed the occasional wild night out, but that didn't usually include one-night stands. I hadn't even let Jimi get past first base.

Despite his firm grasp on my hips, a soft caress started at my collarbone, then swept upward. The man was trailing his lips up my neck. They traced a line of fire up my exposed flesh. Though his mouth didn't latch on, I could sense him inhaling me as if I were a kind of drug.

Then his grasp on me turned painful. Still, there was only the barest, fluttering contact of his lips on my throat, despite his almost violent grip. Why did his bruising hold send more wetness to my center?

"You want me to fuck you right here on the dance floor?" he asked against my ear. "Where that poor idiot can see?"

I tried to pull away, but he held me fast, and if I were honest, I didn't struggle that hard.

He continued to speak low, hypnotizing me as I craved each word after the next. "I would lift your leg and let that stiletto dig into my shoulder while lapping up that honey nectar between your legs, to let everyone here know the queen you are."

A groan ripped out of my throat, and my panties were officially a slip-and-slide. Still, I protested. "I don't want them to know who I am."

Suddenly, I was afraid he did. I was afraid he knew my family and maybe their friends.

A picture of me rubbing against some stranger out at a dive bar with cheap drinks in my stomach would give the press a heyday.

My brain screamed that coming out had been a bad idea. My uncle worked too hard for me to ruin things for him.

Still, my hips swayed in time with the man behind me. I couldn't break from his spell, though that nasty thread of fear wound its way through me.

One of his hands slid up my ribcage, resting just below my breast. I ached for it to go higher. "Nobody knows who you are, though, do they? You make sure of that."

I couldn't tell if I was being seduced or threatened. If this guy thought he could blackmail me, he had another thing coming. Trying to turn my head again, I needed this charade to end. "Do I know you?"

His fingers grasped my cheeks as he pressed his lips against the sensitive shell of my ear. "You don't know me," he rasped, accusatorily, as if he were referring to something far deeper than addressing whether we were strangers or not.

Copper hit my tongue and I instantly sobered. He gripped my face too hard, and my teeth cut the inside of my mouth.

I stiffened as I felt his hardness against my back. Despite my arousal, I realized I'd engaged with a totally unhinged lunatic. I needed to get the hell out of this and fast.

Before I could think of a way to extract myself, cold air replaced where his body just was. I turned around but there was no trace of the man who'd held me captive a second ago.

I was left panting, with chaotic thoughts of fear and arousal, underscored by a deep pit of curiosity.

Viet trotted over to me on her impossibly high heels, with two drinks in her hand and a clutch wedged under one arm. In her binding, strapless dress, her sleeve tattoos were on display. She looked off in the direction I was searching.

"Who was that hottie with a body?" Viet asked, holding a fresh drink out to me.

I took a drink of the cold liquid, but it only highlighted the fever running rampant through me.

"Nobody," I said, as I realized my hands were shaking. My stomach somersaulted, and the press of the people closed in around me.

Setting my mostly full drink down on a nearby ledge, I

yelled over the music. "I'm not feeling so hot. I'm going head out."

Viet gave me a pouty face, as if to argue. But something about my expression must have let me off the hook. She gave me a one-armed hug and instructed me to text her when I got home.

I grabbed my bag and helmet from behind the bar, then changed in the bathroom back into my jeans so I could ride home.

I didn't feel at ease again until I was riding through the streets of downtown Denver, the wind whipping around me. It helped cool my skin, erase the hot brand of his intense gaze and possessive touch. I was just letting off steam, letting him get so close. No different than dancing and having fun in a dive bar.

So why couldn't I stop wishing I got a closer view of his face? I got the strangest feeling that if I got to see the stranger in proper light, look him in the eyes, I'd get back something I lost.

6

KAT

WHAT THE ACTUAL FUCK HAD THAT BEEN ABOUT? WAS I SO desperate to avoid New England that I was willing to self-sabotage?

Good job, Kat. Now let's go find another sexy-looking maniac to give you the hottest night of your life before chopping you up into itty bitty pieces.

Still, the guy left me utterly hot and bothered. The vibration of the powerful bike between my legs had me itching to get to my bedroom and break out my "assistant" to work off this buildup.

Thankfully, no one ever asked to meet my assistant when I said I had a meeting with her. Because she was purple, vibrated, didn't ask questions, and delivered on my every whim.

I was pulled out of my horny thoughts by the sight of a lone figure ambling along the side of the road. It looked like a girl around nine years old. A little girl was wandering the downtown streets of Denver at one in the morning?

That was definitely not right.

What the hell was a little girl doing out here on her own? Worst-case scenarios cascaded through my mind.

The girl wore a dirty nightgown, and her long, dark hair hung around her face. I hadn't seen anyone else around for several blocks, but this was not the safest side of town. She staggered slightly as if exhausted.

As my bike rolled past her, I could have sworn I heard words filter through my helmet.

"Help me."

Before I could turn the bike around or pull over, I blinked and the little girl appeared in front of me on the road. I swerved hard to avoid hitting her. The bike slid onto its side. I hit the ground hard and went tumbling. My head knocked about in my helmet as I rolled across the pavement. Hot pain scraped against my skin as the pavement battled my exposed flesh.

Stars danced before my eyes. I blinked them away from where I lay on the ground. I wasn't sure if I had blacked out for long, or if it had been mere minutes since I'd gone careening off the bike. I stumbled to my feet.

Relief swept through me as I counted my blessings. Thank god, I hadn't been crunched under my own bike. Checking my body, I found several angry, red scrapes that stung like fire. I was shaken, but all my bits were intact. No broken bones, no deep wounds.

The helmet felt too tight around my swollen, sweaty

head. With a hard yank, I pulled it off, but kept it in hand. Turning around, I found the little girl standing on the sidewalk where I'd first spotted her.

Did I have too many drinks? I thought I'd been fine to drive, but how did I not see the little girl in the road a moment ago?

The girl's head was downcast, hair still covering her face. I started toward her.

"Hey hun, are you alright?" I called out from several yards away.

"Help me." The girl's warbling plea echoed around me, causing me to halt.

An icy drip drip drip of dread started in my stomach.

Something was very, very wrong. Goosebumps rose along my body under my riding gear.

The girl's head lifted with the audible creak of bones, and panic hit me like a freight train. Her fingertips looked as though they'd been dipped in tar.

Gray tinted her near-translucent skin, and her eyes were completely black.

I realized too late that I faced a demon.

I turned to run back to my bike, but only got a few steps before I was tackled to the ground. Surprisingly strong arms rolled me over onto my back. The demonic girl sat backward on my chest. She started to rip at my clothes with incredible strength. In no time, she'd shredded the tough fabric of my jeans. Constantly shifting her weight and position, her fingers dug past the fabric and into my thigh, scratching away flesh and tearing into me. I cried out as pain flooded my body.

Her nails were sharp and relentless as she ripped into me.

Whirling around, so she was sitting on my hips, facing

me now, she tore at my shirt.

If I didn't stop her, she wouldn't stop digging until she'd pulled my insides out. A shock of adrenaline sparked in me.

Before she could dig into the soft part of my belly with her insistent, greedy fingers, I grabbed her wrists and hooked my leg across my body between us. I launched my leg and jettisoned her back and off me.

"Thank you, sensei," I mumbled. My Krav Maga teacher had a striking resemblance to that movie action-star, Jason Statham, and worked me until I was pouring buckets of sweat. I owed him for that little move.

But the demon girl was on me again in less than a second. She grabbed my head and slammed it into the pavement. Pain exploded in my brain and sent shockwaves out to the rest of my body. My vision turned black.

Then her weight was gone.

The copper taste of blood and fear flooded my mouth. What was she going to do to me next?

I stared up at the cloudy night sky. I should move. I needed to get up and run, right now, or I would die. But I couldn't force myself to. Shock froze my muscles and my breathing had turned shallow. Pain, hot and bright, radiated from my inner thigh and pounded at the back of my skull.

Somehow, I gathered enough gumption to move my hand down to the painful region of my thigh. My fingers met with sticky warmth. I stopped breathing altogether. It was my own blood. My brain tumbled into a mess of thoughts. I knew the femoral artery was roughly there, but I couldn't remember if it was in only one leg or both. How long would it take for me to bleed out?

Why wasn't she back? Had she left me to die?

An ice-cold raindrop splatted on my face. Then another.

I would have shut my eyes, but I feared closing them

meant I was done for, so I blinked against the slow but steady drip from the sky. My vision darkened for a moment as the pain at the back of my head continued to radiate.

The sound of crunching gravel neared. Someone or something large approached.

"Fucking hell," I heard a man's voice mutter.

Then I was looking up into the steely eyes of the man from the club, his head protecting my face from the falling drops of ice water. The sheen of a long, ornate sword winked at me from his hand.

Black ichor was splattered across his grim face. Then I felt his hands run up my legs, and I whimpered.

"Am I going to—" Then I stopped because how would he know? And maybe I didn't want to know. Where was my phone? My hands began to pat the ground around me, searching for my phone.

I fought to stay conscious. I wasn't sure if it was the shock, the pain, or my breathless panting, but darkness began to cloud my vision.

The man grasped my hand. "You are going to be fine." His eyes shone with hot fervor. As if he would dive into hell itself to grab me by the scruff of my neck and drag me back to Earth if I dared leave him.

I swallowed, confused by the rioting feelings inside me. It was all too much, too intense. I didn't know him and I may have survived a monster only to fall into the hands of an even bigger predator. "Please don't hurt me," I begged just above a whisper.

The shock and sadness that washed over his face sent me spiraling back into time. To the face of a little boy who stood over my father's prone, bloody body.

My last thought before the darkness swallowed me up was... *he came back.*

7

————

GATSBY

, I THOUGHT, EVEN AS I LAID KAT ON my couch. I sneered at the sight of her there.

Not because I was repulsed with her. Never.

I was disgusted with myself. To see the princess splayed out on my broken, discarded furniture, hurt... it was wrong. She should lay on sheets of silk far away from this place and men like me.

The yellowed wallpaper of the abandoned apartment peeled down halfway. The floor creaked like a wailing ghost being murdered all over again, and there were holes in the walls that small children could climb through. But this place barely smelled of mildew, and the mattress was the cleanest I'd rested my head on in months.

I lowered myself to her feet and gently spread her legs. My knife slipped through the remaining tatters of her clothes like they were made of butter. My nostrils flared as the copper smell of her blood hit my senses. I went on to cut away her pants. The inner seam of her jeans had a growing dark spot of blood.

They were already ruined from where the She had clawed through Kat's thigh.

The pieces of fabric dropped at my side. It was a deep gash, but she wasn't in danger of bleeding out. I went about cleaning it with as much clinical precision as I could. The effort it took not to do anything else, while the girl from my dreams lay before me in only a pair of pink panties with a bow at the top.

The gash was dangerously close to the edge of that sugary pair of underwear, and I stiffened in my pants. For the thousandth time, I recognized the universe was punishing me.

I may not be a hero, but I sure as hell wasn't the guy who would do anything to a girl while she was unconscious. Pushing aside my carnal impulses, I focused on treating her as if she were any other no-name civilian.

Not that I'd had much experience with that. Usually, my job was to make sure they were untreatable.

With her pants gone, I could discern the depth of the cut. It needed stitches.

"Fuck," I muttered after examining the coloring on her gash.

"Wh-what are you doing?" Kat asked in a groggy voice.

"I need you to stay calm," I instructed.

Her head whipped about as she took in the dilapidated

surroundings. "Stay calm? Stay calm even though a psychopath with boundary issues kidnapped me and took me back to some abandoned building?"

My heart dropped. Right before she'd lost consciousness, I saw a spark in her eyes, as if she remembered who I was.

Not that it mattered. I was nothing to her. I was nobody to anybody and that's how I liked it.

Her hair was mussed in the most annoyingly attractive way. Then Kat took in her pant-less state, and how I kneeled between her legs, and she made to jump away from me.

"Oh, hell no, you psycho rapist," she cried.

When she tried to get up, I laid a hand on her lower stomach and firmly pushed her back down. Kat groaned and her eyes fluttered close. I showed up in time to see the She knock Kat's head on the pavement with a sickening crack. She'd have a headache for the next couple days, but she'd live.

I needed to deliver the bad news. "The She poisoned you."

"Who she?" Her eyes flew open again. They were wild with fear. She went back to trying to fight me to get up, her eyes closing against the pain in her skull as she continued to buck. Even if she weren't weak right now, I could easily overpower her.

Kat feared me.

I tried to push past the ugly feeling that coiled in my gut at that. "The little girl. It was a demon, remember? They are called the She. The She were once little girls who slaughtered their families or friends. Their souls became damned, and they turned into demons. And this particular She slashed you with something nasty on her fingers and..." I took a deep breath. "I need to suck the poison out."

Kat stilled abruptly, eyes turning round and wide. "What?" she asked in a low, measured voice. I could tell she hoped she heard me wrong.

I spoke slowly and succinctly, so she would understand. "I need to suck out the poison or you will fall into a fever dream and die. Got it, princess?"

"I'm not a princess. Take me to a hospital." Her voice snapped like a rubber band.

I ground my teeth. "There isn't time for that. And they wouldn't know what to do. I've dealt with this before. You need to trust me."

A nervous cackle shot out of her throat. "Trust you? Trust the scary, weirdo guy in the club who got physically aggressive with me and took me back to this..." Her eyes traveled around the dump and became even more fearful.

I could see her climbing toward hysteria.

"Do you want to die?" I sneered, hoping my biting edge would cut through whatever tornado of fear was taking hold of her.

Kat's jaw clicked shut and she shook her head. Dark circles appeared under her rapidly dilating eyes. Redness crept into the whites around her dark orbs.

Shit, the poison was working faster than I anticipated.

"Then lie back and let me do the work, princess," I ordered.

My aggressive approach worked for about a second, but then her flight-or-fight kicked back in and she struggled to get away. I palmed her stomach down again, slamming her hips back into the couch. Then I wound my arms around her legs, spreading them, and dropped my mouth to her inner thigh before she could try to get away again.

Each flavor hit my tongue in separate waves. The salty

sweetness of her skin, the copper of her blood, and the bitterness of the She's poison.

Kat's fingers grabbed my hair as if to try and yank me off. She never pulled, but she continued to wriggle under me.

"I can—I can feel it burning in my blood," she whimpered.

Anger and fear welled in me. I sucked harder. Then turning my head to the side, I spit the ichor straight on the ground. Then I latched my mouth back to the wound.

I hated how much I enjoyed being between her legs like this while she suffered and fought. I truly was a monster. As I inhaled the musk of her sex, my cock hardened almost painfully.

The thought of moving two inches to the left, hooking a finger around those pink panties, and exploring the forbidden temptations there assailed me. I wanted to touch, taste, her soft wetness until she screamed my name.

Kat bucked again as if she knew my nasty, dirty thoughts.

I was a bad, bad man.

Winding my arms around her thighs tighter, I spread her legs farther so I could get in there and suck harder, faster. Her flexibility gave my shoulders ample room to crowd in.

Fuck. I was rock hard now.

I forced myself to shove aside my primal urges for the irresistible woman I kneeled before. Clinical precision was needed. I'd ruined her life, so it was a small ask that I didn't fuck with her any further.

I worked hard and fast, sucking and spitting out the bitterness, until I was only left with the salt and copper of her skin and blood. I pulled back and wiped my mouth with the back of my hand.

Kat had relaxed back, her eyes closed, skin covered in a

sheen of sweat.

I pushed away from her, almost violently. Then I stalked to the other side of the room, so I didn't have to look at her all spread out like an invitation.

Kat wasn't meant for me, and I needed to remember that. My fingers pulled at my hair, as I raged against my own idiocy.

When I turned around, I found she had passed out again.

I needed to get her gone. Out of this place and back in her pristine castle before I could fuck things up any further.

It didn't take long to stitch her up and bandage the scrapes on her arms and legs before I slid a pair of my sweats on her. She didn't wake, even as I cradled her in my arms on my bike, roaring back to her place.

Avoiding all security cameras, I managed to get her back up to her room. Locked windows and doors weren't enough to keep me out.

The black and white dog caught up with me and escorted me to Kat's bed. I'd met her mutt years ago, and after an hour straight of staring at each other, the dog growling low in its throat, it suddenly relaxed and came over to me, licking my hands.

I laid Kat in her own bed and pulled the sheets up to her shoulders. Her normally golden complexion had paled, but I knew she would be alright. The dog jumped onto the bed to lay on Kat's feet. The canine looked back and forth between me and her master with baleful brown eyes as if silently asking if she would be alright.

"She'll be fine," I assured the dog.

Fantastic, now I was as foolish as a civilian, talking to a dog like it could understand me.

Still, the dog laid its head down as if I'd appeased it.

My hand hovered over Kat's hair, as I was tempted to stroke it. My heart squeezed almost violently as I fought the impulse.

Don't touch her. You kill everything you touch.

The voice in my head sounded suspiciously like my old master's. My fingers curled into my palm and I whirled around, striding back toward the balcony.

"You're him, aren't you?" a small voice asked behind me.

My shoulders tensed as I stopped, but I didn't turn around.

"You are the boy who came to my window. The one who visited every night in secret until that night I found you over my father's body." Kat's voice thickened with emotion.

Closing my eyes, I cursed myself. I'd tried to keep her eyes averted from my face at the club. It had been so long, but I feared she would recognize me.

But maybe I wanted her to see me. Because when her eyes fell on me, they didn't stay surface-level. They cut straight through all my defenses, like she saw everything inside me. That's how it felt that first night she found me in her tree.

No, I didn't want that. I didn't want her to see the dark, ugly things inside me. So, I planned to stay far away, but she proved to be too enticing tonight, and I had to touch her, inhale her in that club. She smelled like every temptation rolled in sugar. But I still walked away.

Then the She attacked, and I couldn't stand by and do nothing.

Turning my gaze to the floor off to my left, I ground out, "I'm not that boy."

The bed squeaked as she readjusted herself. "Stop talking in riddles. I know who you are. And I've been waiting to ask you something for over ten years."

When I finally turned to face Kat, tears brimmed in her eyes. Her back now sagged against the bed frame where she sat. The dog stayed lying across her feet.

A lance pierced my heart at the sight of Kat so vulnerable.

"Did you..." Her voice broke. Then she rolled her shoulders back, bracing herself. "Did you kill my father?"

I stared at her, letting the silence stretch out too long between us. Her desperation filled the air, and it choked me.

Master Wu's voice snaked in my brain again. *Everything you touch dies. That is your curse, which we have transformed into our gift.*

"No," I finally said before starting toward the balcony.

"Your name," she rushed to say as if in a panic. As if she would perish if she didn't know this very second.

I paused, meaning to tell her she didn't need to know. That knowing my name could get her killed or worse. But a dark, secret, selfish part of me wanted her to know my name.

"Gatsby. My name is Gatsby."

Then before she could ask me anything else, I left. The doors shut behind me, and I easily scaled the tree back down, hoping she'd stay in bed.

She needed the rest, and I needed to get away from her.

Tonight, I'd get on my bike and drive out of the city and never come back. Forget Kat, and everyone I knew in this damn city.

Even as I thought it, I knew I was lying to myself. I couldn't leave. Not yet, not until I knew Kat was safe. The She had nearly tore her body apart, but I had to protect Kat from the demon who wanted her.

And I had to do everything I could to make sure I wasn't the one who tarnished her soul.

8

KAT

My eyes opened at dawn's first light. At first, I'd thought it had all been a dream. But I knew it was all real when I found myself wearing sweatpants that weren't my own, and bandages covering my arms.

Bear lay on my feet and regarded me with evident concern. I swear that dog was scary intelligent. When I tried to move, he immediately got up so I could more easily move. He jumped off the bed and sat down, as if waiting for me to get my wits about me.

Getting out of bed, I moved carefully so as not to jostle myself into any more pain, but I was surprised to find myself largely pain free. My bag sat on my desk, with everything still in it.

Not that I thought the boy, turned impossibly hot scary man, would rob me after all that, but I couldn't rule anything out.

As I ran the shower, warming the water, I took a peek under my bandages. The stinging, raw scrapes of last night were completely gone. I peeled back the one on my inner thigh and found stitches, but the skin had already knitted back together, and the skin was bright red in the shape of a slash. I expected my head to pound after all the trauma it had taken yesterday, but there wasn't even a trace of a headache.

I grabbed my nail scissors and easily snipped the stitches and pulled them out.

Had I imagined last night and bandaged up imaginary wounds? No, I'd definitely crashed my bike. I should be scratched to shit. Or at the very least, I should feel the remnants of a headache from where my head had been cracked against the ground.

Burying my fingers in my hair, I tried to make sense of things. But it felt like I'd undergone several bouts of whiplash. As soon as I saw the man at the club, he practically melted off my panties, before getting too aggressive with me on the dance floor, preventing me from looking at his face while promising to do impossibly sexual things to me in public. Then he disappeared, only to show up again when I was attacked by a little demon girl asking for my help who almost disemboweled me.

Then I woke up in what looked like a condemned apartment building, with no pants on and a grown man claiming he had to suck the poison out from my wound, or I'd die. Then he sucked on my inner thigh, dangerously close to my center, sending a myriad of intense and confusing feelings spiraling through my body.

My fingers tightened in my hair as I began to rock back and forth on the toilet seat. Steam swirled around me. Oh god, the feel of his mouth on me. I shut my eyes tight against the tumult of heat in my body that started shooting straight toward my center again.

Gatsby never looked up at me, just spread my legs, held me down, and sucked on me like there was no tomorrow.

Had my blood not begun to burn, making me queasy, I might have suggested he move a couple inches over and...

Another flood of heat in my body had me scrubbing at my face to stop the rest of that fantasy from playing out.

And though my gut recognized him in the club, it wasn't until after he took me safely home that I could admit to myself who he was. The boy who may have killed my father.

No, Gatsby said he hadn't killed him.

What was I supposed to make of all this?

That I needed to march into my Krav Maga dojo and demand a refund. I'd been preparing to defend myself, and I'd completely and utterly failed to do so. Aside from that one little move I pulled, I absolutely choked in the moment. I'd been going for years to feel like I could protect myself. But that sense of security I'd worked so hard to build was ripped away from me like a piece of sheer fabric.

Yep. That's what I would do, I decided, as I stepped under the scalding stream of water. I would blame my sensei for what happened and forget everything else.

It was called compartmentalization, and it was all I could handle right now.

I slept in too late to greet my uncle and cousins at the breakfast table, but I got a text reminder from my uncle's assistant that tonight was a garden party gala at the home of one of his wealthier supporters, and he expected to see me there.

When I went out through the garage to let Bear out, I was surprised to find my bike parked in its usual spot. Albeit scratched up on one side, but it was in one piece. How the hell had he gotten it in here without being seen? There were cameras and guards everywhere.

After feeding and loving on Bear for an appropriate amount of time, I resolved to get out. If I didn't now, I might never leave the safety of this house again.

I decided to take my car. My insides quaked at the memory of sliding on my bike.

Once I got to the studio, I pulled my easel into a corner where no one could see what I was painting. With my headphones covering my ears, I blocked out the world and sunk into the heavy beats of my music. My brush worked against the canvas in blues and blacks with occasional gold highlights, bringing to life the image I felt burning in my soul. It needed to be made physical, or the image would incinerate me from the inside out.

Viet eventually showed up, but she was careful not to try and take a peek at my canvas, knowing how private I could get. She asked how the rest of my night had been and she'd been worried when I didn't text her. I played it off perfectly as though nothing eventful happened.

Maybe you should tell her? About the demon? About the man who saved you. About the boy who visited you as a child?

I immediately flung that idea out the window with the baby and the bathwater. I learned long ago not to share. Viet was a fun friend, but I wasn't sure I could trust her with all the scary whackadoo stuff going on.

The day went on almost painfully normal, though my world felt tilted on its axis. But there was no time to call my therapist and sort things out. I had responsibilities.

When I got home, I threw on an evening gown. Emerald green and silk with thin straps and a slit up one leg. It was one of my favorites, even though it was a little on the risqué side for the garden party. I pulled my hair into an elegant updo and slid on some stilettos knowing the garden was well paved. I wanted to feel my power and not cower in a corner. After last night, it was important I reminded myself I could handle anything, or fear could infect and mold me. I refused to be molded by fear, especially in an age where monsters were real.

An hour later at the party, I was already exhausted from playing the vapid and shallow game of "How are you?" and fielding too many inquiries about me looking forward to law school. I hadn't even applied yet and everyone kept cementing my future until it felt like it would be the concrete block that drowned me.

My uncle seemed pleased, though, and my cousins and Dave and Gabe were completely in their element. They were heavily involved in my uncle's politics, and Dave would soon follow in his footsteps. Gabe's girlfriend was present as usual. They'd been together for two years now. Molly Kramer was petite, blonde hair, porcelain skin and light blue eyes. She rarely spoke, always showed up in the perfect outfit that was modest and elegant. We were always polite to each other, but she usually let Gabe speak for her.

I retreated to a far corner of the garden with a flute of champagne to recharge my emotional battery. As I wondered if it was too soon to make a quiet yet graceful exit, I felt a presence join me.

Heat prickled along my skin and raced down my body in an almost automatic Pavlovian reaction of arousal.

"What are you doing here?" I asked in a flat voice.

Gatsby stepped out from the shadows cast by the tall wall of hedges. "You are in danger."

"You are in danger of me calling security to remove you from this party," I said matter-of-factly, before sipping my champagne.

Gatsby claimed not to have killed my father. But I didn't trust him.

Yes, you do, a voice whispered inside me.

I tried to brush that stupid voice off.

"You need protection," Gatsby said.

Finally, I turned to face him. He fit in about as well as a Doberman wearing a kitten costume. Though he was in suit jacket and slacks, he'd skipped the tie, leaving the top several buttons undone, revealing his neck tattoos.

The vision of him as a child overlapped with his grown self, and again I had the sense I was face to face with the original lost boy. But I wasn't Wendy, and life wasn't a fairytale.

He sported nearly worn-out boots instead of dress shoes, and a sword hung over his back in its sheath. Not that it was as unusual to see people packing weapons since the dimension to hell opened, but our security usually favored guns.

Even then, everyone knew bullets sometimes weren't enough.

I couldn't believe Gatsby had gotten in here without being pegged as a party crasher. If someone attended one of these things in less than a thousand-dollar suit, they were panned in whispers for weeks.

I turned away to keep from drooling over the strip of his inked, exposed chest and neck. Gatsby didn't belong, but he somehow managed to look like a rugged sex god who could lay anyone out and destroy them in a single thrust.

I shrugged off the disturbing yet enticing thought.

"I take care of myself just fine," I insisted. "Last night was a fluke. I am perfectly capable of defending myself and staying safe. I'd gone a little on the wild side last night, but my late nights out are coming to an end anyway."

My stomach dropped as I fast-forwarded my life into sitting in some gray lecture hall, listening about the difference between criminal and civil cases.

Suddenly angry, I poked him in the chest to keep him at arm's length. "So next time you think I need saving, just cruise right on."

Instead of being pushed away, his warm, dry hands covered my mine. They were callused, but smooth. He drew near until he was practically standing over me. Sharp gray eyes pinned me while his scent wrapped around me, making my knees weak. "You wanted me to come save you."

I scoff. "Didn't you hear me? I don't need saving."

The serious expression that swept over his face left me feeling both hollow and uncertain. I tried to pull away, but he wouldn't let me.

The boy who destroyed my world stood in front of me, and instead of flying at him in a violent rage, I found myself captured by him.

My voice came out quieter than I liked. "Next time I won't be caught off guard, and I'll bring demon repellent."

I was half-joking. The infomercials claimed Demon No-No spray was the answer. But I'd count on something a little sharper. At the very least, I'd be back in the dojo tomorrow.

He bowed his head closer, and his scent washed over

me. "I mean you wanted me to save you from that idiot on the dance floor."

"He seemed like a perfectly nice guy," I countered, though I struggled to swallow. The heat of his hands engulfed mine. I could smell him... a mixture of sex and home. It was criminal to smell that good.

"No," he rasped. "You were too good for him. He moved like a clumsy oaf and you tolerated him. You wanted someone to come meet you on your level. Someone who can keep up with you, princess."

My protest at him calling me princess again died in my throat as he leaned in farther. Lips parted, eyes trained on mine, I was certain he was about to kiss me. I could practically taste the cinnamon on his lips. Had he been chewing gum?

"Why did you say those things to me on the dance floor?" I managed to get out. The dirty image he'd painted played on repeat in my head all day. The one where my stiletto dug in his shoulder while he lapped at my sex in front of everyone.

Something in his gaze faltered, as if I'd thrown him off. "It was a cover. Meant to distract you."

I gestured with my glass at him. "You're an absolute shit liar, you know that?"

"Kitty Kat," a male voice cut through the intimacy like a butcher knife.

I jerked back and out of Gatsby's hold.

Gatsby held his wrist and took a step, his expression flattening.

So engrossed, I hadn't noticed the three men approach.

"Jimi," I acknowledged while smoothing down my dress. His friends Alan and Ross were with him, as always. They were all built with thick muscles since they'd played on the same rugby and polo teams since middle school. Alan and Ross had shorter necks and were even stockier than Jimi.

The blond, freckled man shot Gatsby a suspicious glare as he spoke to me. "Who's this? I don't believe we've met before." The grin Jimi gave Gatsby was purely plastic as he held out his hand.

"Um this is..." *This was the boy who I couldn't decide if he was saving me or ruining my life whenever I saw him.*

"I'm Gatsby, her bodyguard." Instead of shaking Jimi's hand, Gatsby moved next to me as if to back me up.

I shot Gatsby a look that let him know we'd be talking about his chosen title later.

Jimi closed his fingers into a fist and dropped his arm with an almost predatory smile now. "I didn't realize her body needed guarding. And from what I just saw, it looks like she might need some protection from you."

Gatsby started forward, but I stopped him with a hand on his chest. I didn't know how Gatsby defeated that little demon girl or if maybe he just chased her off. But Jimi was pure brute muscle, and the last thing my uncle or this party needed was a brawl.

"Did you need something, Jimi?" I asked with saccharine sweetness, redirecting the conversation.

Finally peeling his gaze off Gatsby, Jimi shot me an earnest look. "Yes, actually. I was hoping for a moment alone with you."

Internally, I sighed, but I didn't want a scene, so I nodded. My hand was still on Gatsby's hard, warm chest. "I'll be right back." I hoped he caught the plea in my eyes not to follow and not to make a scene in my absence.

Jimi escorted me over to the majestic mermaid where we were out of earshot of anyone. Jimi flashed me a brilliant smile. He would have made Barbie swoon and given Ken a run for his money. He tucked an errant hair behind my ear, in what should have been a romantic gesture, but I felt less than nothing.

The skin along the back of my neck prickled with heat. Gatsby was watching our every move.

"I'm glad to see you here. You look perfect as usual," he flattered.

I managed a half-smile for his benefit, but for some reason it always bothered me to be told I looked or acted perfect. That was oddly what I strived to do and be, but it always hit me wrong when I heard it out loud.

Strangely, I itched to get back to ignoring Gatsby.

Jimi went on, "I know we've been taking things casually, but I think it's time we take the next step."

I stopped a server passing by, exchanging my champagne for a fresh, cold one. I gulped some down to stall, but Jimi patiently waited for me to respond.

"What's the next step?" I finally asked.

"You, me, going official? The tabloids would go nuts, able to graduate from the supposed rumors that we are together to celebrating our union."

"You make it sound like a marriage proposal," I said with a wry laugh.

The smile on his face froze.

Oh. Oh god.

Jimi went on. "Voters will be at the polls soon, and we know how much this would help your uncle."

Going to Harvard Law was one thing, but marry Jimi? We'd done some necking in closets at these boring events, but nothing beyond that. I didn't think of him when I woke up, or when I went to bed. No, a pair of intense gray eyes dominated those moments. Longer than I cared to admit.

A movement caught my eye, and I turned to see my

uncle raise a glass in my direction as others chatted around him. He'd given Jimi his blessing.

Of course he had. Why wouldn't he?

"Jimi," I started. "You are a great guy, but I'm not in love with you."

Unfazed, he shrugged. "We've got chemistry, the rest will come with time."

The champagne in my stomach turned sour and my skin flushed with embarrassment. "I'm sorry Jimi, I... I can't." The wretched feeling hit me full force. I loved my family, they were all I had, but I couldn't do this.

"Kitty Kat," Jimi crooned.

"Don't call me that," I said firmly. I never told him I hated his little nickname. I didn't want to be rude. But right now, I was possessed by a different woman altogether. With Gatsby near, I didn't know what I would do. It both scared and excited me.

Jimi's face darkened. "Is this because of that guy?" He gestured in Gatsby's direction. I turned to see Alan and Ross standing by him as if to prevent him from approaching. He watched me intently, and I had to turn away.

"Not at all, it's just been a lot lately. I'm not ready for anything right now. Not even something casual."

I must have been convincing, because Jimi's stance relaxed. "Of course, I know how hard this week must be for you. The anniversary of—"

"Thanks for understanding," I cut him off before rushing off to greet one of my uncle's supporters as if she were a long-lost aunt.

The evening went on like that. Me flitting from person to person, talking about absolutely nothing. About my future in law, and the close run my uncle was having with his competitor. It was a close race, but they had every confidence in John Hart, who '*always brought heart to the situation.*' My smile was bright, and I said all the right things, but I felt my soul being chipped away into dust.

Meanwhile, Gatsby continued to stalk the perimeter of the party. I could feel him tracking my every move. I pretended to listen to Judge Johnson's story about his infamous case with the priest and the rabbi. It was maybe the tenth time I'd heard it.

"Did you see that guy over there? I think he's a party crasher," a woman said, off to the side.

A group of politicians' wives who were pounding their usual vodka martinis had noticed Gatsby.

The bleached-blonde woman went on. "How did he even get in here, looking like that?"

Another one of the blonde wives overtly licked her lips. "I'd let him in anywhere he wanted."

My eyebrows scrunched at her remark, and the judge took it to be increased interest in his story so he puffed out his chest. But I was keyed in on the martini-guzzling women currently licking their chops at Gatsby. I glanced in his direction to find him lurking at the edge of the garden, like he was hired muscle for the party. If he wanted to blend in, he should at least have a drink in hand.

A dark-haired wife elbowed her. "Jacinda, you must be joking."

Jacinda shook her head, directing a powerful beam of bedroom eyes in Gatsby's direction. "Oh no, I'm not. When I say anywhere, I mean *anywhere*." She gave a throaty laugh.

Gatsby must have felt their probing eyes because he met her gaze over the rim of her glass. Instead of returning her bedroom eyes, his look was meant to cut her down to the knees. But Jacinda was too many martinis in to receive the wordless message.

A redhead who'd gone overboard with the lip fillers chimed in. "He's hot in that blue-collar kind of way, where you know he'd throw you around and lick you in places none of our husbands would be willing."

My spine stiffened. My brain and body warred with the thought of him doing those things to one of these women, tumbled in with the fantasy of him doing those things to me. I couldn't even pretend with the judge anymore, but he had plenty of others nodding and smiling at his tale.

Fantasies aside, I hated how they cheapened Gatsby to some sex object to be used. But that's how the people in these circles were. They pasted on shiny smiles until they could find out what you could do for them. This was the world my family on my father's side had been entrenched in for generations, but sometimes it almost physically hurt to be at these things.

My father said my mother loved the parties, but I mainly had memories of her retreating to the kitchen with the caterers, kicking off her heels, and sharing bits of naan or milk chocolate pieces with me while I sat in her lap.

Jacinda scoffed. "Of course, he only has eyes for the young girl who looks like a Victoria's Secret model. Though she fancies herself some kind of artist, playing with paints like she's Picasso. I don't know why John has indulged her this long. She could at least use her looks to help further his cause instead of finger painting all day long."

I stiffened when I realized they were talking about me. My eyes flew back to the judge, pretending to be engrossed again though I couldn't hear a word he was saying now.

The redhead said, "She's young and beautiful like one of the little knobby-kneed fillies we breed, but *I* could teach him things. Things that would make his toes curl, and hump like a beast."

Unable to take another second, I walked away to get out of earshot. The way they wanted to tear into Gatsby reminded me of a bunch of horny hyenas.

A sick feeling churned in my stomach as their words still followed me. It was true that I'd been approached to do modeling many times, but I far preferred to be behind a canvas in my own world than in front of a camera without my clothes on.

Those women didn't know me. I wasn't finger painting; I had my own gallery show tomorrow.

Still, the imposter syndrome began to snake into my being, infiltrating me with doubt.

Who did I think I was to make art and show it off like I was something? Everyone here thought I was a childish joke.

I'd already known what people thought of me, but hearing it made it even harder to escape.

I looked up and found Gatsby's gaze lasered in on me. He looked at me like he knew. Like he knew the awful things I'd just heard and how desperately lonely it made me. Like he knew I was holding on by a mere thread in a crowd of people who suspected nothing.

The intensity in his eyes cut through the air. It said, I know you are about to fall, but I will catch you and take you away from anything that causes you pain.

It ripped the breath right out of my chest to have my most private torture seen. The ache in my heart doubled.

From the opposite side of the Garden, Gatsby was a magnet. Only he and I could feel the understanding pulsating in the space between. It felt like someone would notice at any moment, but the people around us continued to drink and chat without any concept that the man across the party was rocking my entire foundation simply by seeing me.

It was powerful, addictive, and it took everything in me not to run into his arms and let him take me away from everything. Even myself. Turning my gaze down to the bright pink tulips lining the path, I took in a deep breath, forcing the urge to pass.

When I looked up, Gatsby was gone. Disappeared again. The ache in my belly yawned open, threatening to swallow me.

God, I really was a dumb little helpless girl.

My therapist was going to have a heyday with this one.

But I wouldn't be sharing this. My emotion choked out logic like a WWE wrestler. It was as secret and special as that box that still sat hidden under my bed. I truly had reverted to that romantic little girl who fell for the boy outside her window.

Now the question was, would he show up outside my window again tonight?

9

GATSBY

IT WOULD BE SO EASY TO CUT HER THROAT. TO LET THE warmth of her blood slip over my hands like it had so many times before.

The thought instantly made me ill. I was a sick, twisted bastard.

Kat's champagne-colored silk chemise rode up, revealing her taut stomach, making my mouth water and my fists clench. Her dark hair fanned against the pristine white pillow.

Did something sick inside me want to kill the thing I wanted most of all? Or did I fear that someone or something else could so easily infiltrate her bedroom, melt into the shadows like I had, and take her from this world?

Arm raised over her head, Kat's eyes were tensed around the corners, even in sleep. The same expression of concentration when she was in her studio. Not the moments when she was furiously painting. No, this was the expression she wore when she stared at her canvas for hours without lifting a finger, listening to her music on those absurdly big, pink headphones with cat ears. What I would give to know what she listened to in those moments as she created images in her mind that would transfer to her fingertips.

I didn't create. I destroyed.

And I desperately wanted to know what she locked away in that secret closet. What she created when she worked in the middle of the night, unable to sleep. Kat was careful to keep her back to a corner, hiding her easel. When she was done, she'd lock them away. I hungered to see the innermost secrets of her soul in acrylic color. I'd seen many of her pieces. The portraits done in complex colors, and it made me want to fall into her mind and swim there for ages.

Kat's eyes fluttered open as if she could feel the heat of my gaze. I took a step back farther into the shadows.

With a deep, full-body stretch, she yawned. "I know you're there."

That silk chemise rode even higher and my cock twitched.

Then she sat up in her bed. I emerged from the darkened corner of her room, allowing the moonlight filtering through the French doors to illuminate me. Her knees came up and the sheets fell away.

Where she was barely covered, I was back in my shirt, jeans, and leather jacket. I'd felt ridiculous wearing that suit at the party.

Then Kat's silken shorts rode up, revealing the expanse of her delicious thigh as well as the wound from when she'd been attacked. To my surprise, it was nothing more than a faded mark. She must have removed the stitches herself.

Somewhere at the back of my mind, I was aware that wasn't right. It should have taken at least a week or more to heal to this point. I'd noticed at the party her arms appeared unmarred as well. The scratches all but disappeared.

The question of how circled my mind, but it was quickly drowned out by other desires. The dark pools of her eyes, and glossy part of her lips invited me to do all the bad things I desired in my black heart.

"What are you doing here?" she demanded.

I pushed away my dark fantasies. "Like I said, you are in danger."

She arched an eyebrow as she scanned me from head to toe. "I'll say. There is a strange man in my bedroom." Her tone was biting. "I should call the cops and have you removed."

A half-smile touched my lips. "I don't think you want anyone to get hurt, Kat."

The cavalier tone in the air was sucked from the room, as Kat's expression flattened. "What are you doing here, Gatsby? Are you here to ruin my life again? Because that's what happened last time you showed up. You're like a bad omen, an albatross lurking about, promising to sink my ship."

I couldn't answer her question. The sudden heavy weight in my gut prevented me.

Then Kat was on her feet, padding over to stand in front of me in that absurdly sexy peach sleep set. "And then when you are done, you can leave me again?" Fury vibrated in her tone.

Fuck, why did she smell so goddamn delicious? Like sugared violets. Sleep and anger only intensified the scent. After circling around her for so long, being this close was beyond intoxicating. I wanted to lick up her collar bone to nibble on that perfect earlobe.

Then her accusation penetrated my haze of arousal.

"You're mad I left you?" I asked.

She poked me in the chest with a sharp finger, for the second time tonight. Her eyes suddenly glittered with unshed tears of fury. "You acted like you were my friend. You claim you didn't kill my father, so then why did you leave? Do you know what they did to me after you left? No one believed me. Not about the boy who visited me every night but never showed up on a single ounce of security footage. And no one believed me about the..." The words seemed to die in her throat. With a deep inhale, she pressed on in a lower, gravelly voice, "No one believed I saw a demon."

There was nothing I could say.

Kat averted her gaze from my eyes to stare at my chest. "The state put me in an institution for a while. They said the stress of my dad's murder made me go crazy. Looking back, I see how they couldn't put me in foster care, so they stashed me away where they didn't have to deal with me. Then, the louder I was about what happened, the harder they ground me down. They gave me pills. So many pills, I couldn't do anything but stare at the walls and drool. They said they were making me *comfortable*, but they only trapped me with the memory of that night and that creature. When my uncle showed up to take custody, I'd already been in there two weeks. Eventually my uncle rescued me. He got me released and became my guardian, but it took another week. It felt like an entire lifetime passed in there."

I couldn't help but step in closer to her, but I didn't let

myself touch her. I didn't deserve to touch her. She couldn't understand all the reasons why I couldn't stay. There were so many, they gathered in my throat, choking me with a hundred violent hands. But above all the other reasons was the fact that if I had stayed, I would have obliterated what was left of her life. I wasn't the hero she wanted me to be.

"It was... it was real, wasn't it?" she finally asked, looking up into my eyes. Desperation and need shone out from them, but I could tell she still feared my answer.

"Yes," I murmured. "A demon killed your father. And now I fear it draws near once again, preparing to come for you."

Kat wrapped her arms around her stomach, her back slightly curving as if she could make herself smaller.

"Why?" she asked.

"The demon returns in... cycles." It was the best I could explain it.

"My birthday," she said, her lips barely moving. "It's coming back on my birthday."

"Perhaps, but I'll feel its presence sooner," I confirmed. "And if you are a target of darkness, other beings will sense it too and begin to thirst for you. Like the She."

"It's going to kill me, like it did my father."

"I won't let it," I said, a sudden fierceness in my voice. "It's why I need to stay close to you, Kat. I tried to keep my distance, but if you are going to be safe, I need to be right by your side. Because if it comes for you, I will stop it."

She whirled around and stalked across her room in agitation. Then she paced back to stand in front of me again. Fire shone from her eyes. "You didn't stop it when it killed my father," she said. "What makes you think you can protect me now?"

Before I could answer, she looked away and rubbed her

forehead. "I'm sorry, that's not fair. You were just a kid. We both were."

A dark laugh came out of me. If she only knew what I'd been capable of as a kid.

"What?" she asked.

I leaned in, inches from her face now, with a dangerous leer on my face. "You don't know me. You didn't know me then. And after I finish this demon off, I'm out of here."

She needed to let go of this idea that we were friends. I didn't have friends.

A scowl darkened her face as she faced off against me. "So, you are planning to leave just like last time?"

"That's right, princess. I came here to take care of unfinished business and that's it. I'm not here for you."

"Fine," Kat practically shouted.

"Good," I shot back.

Our lips crashed against each other with heat and fury. I wasn't sure who had moved first, but my hands instantly covered those perfect ass cheeks, pulling her to me. She tasted like sin, salvation, and honey. The heat of her mouth scalded all the way down to my black soul and lit me up with red passion.

Kat grabbed my hair and fought my mouth, her tongue scraping against my teeth. Fuck, why did I feel like I was drowning in her? My cock pressed painfully hard against my jeans. The coolness of her silk chemise contrasted against the delectable warmth of her skin.

I still remembered the intoxicating scent of her sex when I'd been saving her life. The sensation of needing her turned agonizing. I grabbed the hair at the base of her skull and backed her up to the bed, punishing her with my mouth.

Punishing her for what I couldn't have. For what I was.

For all the unforgivable dark things I'd done. How dare she let me touch her. Didn't she know I could turn her soul black too?

Kat moaned and whimpered under my onslaught, but she didn't push me away.

Anger fused with desire. I broke from her perfect fucking mouth and made my way down the column of her elegant neck.

Why didn't she tell me to stop? She needed to tell me to stop. To order me the fuck out of her life.

Even as I sucked at a sensitive spot between her neck and collarbone that made her buck and whine like an animal, I knew it wouldn't matter. I'd been fooling myself thinking I could leave her to her fate—to the darkness that could swallow her up.

And for some goddamn reason I believed myself to be the lesser evil right now.

"Tell me to stop," I growled against her skin.

Another needy whine vibrated from her throat as she pushed my leather jacket off my shoulders. It fell to the floor.

One of my hands found its way under her chemise top to press against her bare stomach. My fingertips dipping below the elastic of her shorts.

"Tell me to stop," I repeated louder, growing angrier that she wouldn't stop me. That she was forcing me to rely on my own willpower. Around her, it melted into nothingness, leaving me out of control.

Kat's eyes fluttered open to meet mine, a message emanating from them loud and clear.

No. Don't stop.

"You think this is a game?" I demanded. My hand

burrowed lower until my fingers parted her slick lower lips. She gasped and arched her back.

"Fuck," I ground out, as my hips bucked of their own accord as I imagined sinking my hardness into the inviting heat my fingertips played with.

"You think you are safe with me?" I asked, wanting to prove her wrong. "You need to learn I'm not to be trusted with your body."

"I thought you were here to protect it?" she threw at me in a glib tone. Even as she thrust her hips up, trying to get me to go deeper. A challenge flashed in her eyes.

"One last chance, princess," I warned, the last thread of my control fast unraveling. My finger tapped at her opening, and she shuddered.

"Or what?" She bit her swollen bottom lip, and it undid me.

"Fine," I snarled. I pushed her back onto the bed and ripped away both her bottoms and panties in one quick motion.

Shock barely registered on her face, before I grabbed her top and pulled it up over her arms, then bunched it at her wrists, using it as a restraint.

The princess squirmed, naked, splayed out on the bed before me. Her body was taut, her golden skin shimmering in the low light. Wanton, and the absolute most tempting sight I had ever seen in my goddamn life.

From those perfect brown nipples, to the tempting dark patch of curls between her thighs, she was every temptation known to man or monster. Her sex shimmered with moisture. Moisture I'd already spread with my fingers. I stuck my index and middle finger in my mouth, sucking them clean of her salty, feminine taste.

Her eyes rounded and a whimper escaped her throat.

Fuck, I was seconds from losing it in my pants. But I had to teach her a lesson.

"Take off your shirt," she requested in a husky voice.

A dry laugh escaped me. "You're not in control here anymore, princess. You should have told me to stop when you had a chance. Now you are going to learn what a bad man I can be when you don't keep me at arm's length."

I flipped her body over, further twisting her wrists in the chemise-turned-restraint. Bent over the edge of the bed, she was completely at my mercy. I kicked her legs a part, exposing her perfect ass and slick opening.

Unable to help myself, I dragged my fingers up her opening again before bringing them to my mouth to suck on them audibly. She jerked at the sound.

Then I was back to massaging that sexy opening I couldn't take my eyes off. I kept my ministrations shallow no matter how she moaned or tried to push back into me.

"More. Please more," she begged.

A slap rang through the air, my hand stinging from the contact with her ass. She let out a surprised squeal. Even in the low light, I could see a blush on her perfect bronze cheek.

Kat stilled, and I went back to playing with her opening that grew visibly slicker by the second. Mesmerized, I spread that wetness up between the valley of her ass cheeks.

"Wh-what are you doing?" she asked, fear suddenly present in her voice.

"Taking whatever the fuck I want, princess." Then I pushed a finger into that tight rosebud. It tightened against me, but I continued to wiggle my finger and work her own wetness into the opening.

She hadn't believed me when I said I was a bad man.

I'd make her believe.

10

KAT

YET AGAIN, MY BRAIN MARVELED AT HOW THE FUCK I'D gotten into this position with someone so clearly unhinged. Fears and thoughts about cleanliness raced through my head, but I'd showered right before I'd slipped into bed.

You're not actually concerned about the welcome mat you put out for your ass, are you? a critical part of my mind yelled. *This is wrong! Good girls don't do this.*

I had to stop him somehow.

Then that finger pushed against my tight muscles and my pussy clenched up as though it had been hit by an electric zap.

Sweat broke out on my brow and I panted. I couldn't tell if it was from fear or excitement.

Gatsby continued to work his finger in and out of my most private opening, going deeper and deeper.

It vaguely occurred to me to be grateful my bedroom was on the opposite side of the house from everyone else, because the sounds that came out of me were unrecognizable.

Holy fuck, did I just gurgle?

Gatsby's finger dragged against a spot that caused my pussy to tighten up hard even as moisture released in a torrent.

"Do you think a good boy would do this to you?" Gatsby rasped. I saw the already impressive bulge against his pants, and wished he were naked and pounding into me.

"Do you think that guy in the club would? Or that freckled fool at the party would toy with your sweet little asshole until you broke like a naughty slut who is dying for a cock to fill her?"

My hips jerked and a low moan escaped me. Why was it that when he said that I wanted him even more?

I should have been disgusted, outraged. But nothing he did hurt, not even his verbal barbs. They only let me sink into being a girl who succumbed to pleasure no matter how it came.

"You are going to regret not telling me to stop. You are going to regret ever showing me that perfect little pussy of yours."

The hand holding my tied-up hands released its grip. Before I could try to turn over, he pressed me down, spreading my cheeks and did the unthinkable.

His tongue circled my back opening.

It was so wrong. It felt so good.

Then a couple fingers finally penetrated my dripping pussy and I practically screamed as he pumped them into me while worshipping me at my forbidden hole. His tongue dipped in and out, making me go crazy.

The sensation overwhelmed me. In seconds, I came harder than I ever had in my life. I was left panting and sweating.

When Gatsby finally stopped and pulled away, he landed a sound slap against my swollen pussy. I jerked, a mini orgasm immediately triggered by his rough treatment.

But I felt so alive, so uninhibited, so impossibly sexy, my skin hummed with the knowledge that he would eat me up if he could.

Realizing I'd been freed, I rolled over and chucked the chemise from my wrists. I sat up on the bed, looking up at the man standing before me. Still fully clothed, he looked like a dark angel, glaring down at me. His hand rubbed against the bulge in his pants. His mouth glistened with my desire, and he made a point of slowly licking his lips.

On my feet in a second, I grabbed the bottom of his shirt and pulled it over his head. It wasn't enough. I wanted him in me. Balls deep, until I could feel him at the back of my throat from the inside.

Kat, who even are you right now?

I didn't care, he shook something loose in me and it made me bold.

Gatsby stood before me in only his jeans that rode low. I desperately wanted to drag my tongue along the deep cuts of his hips, and up the hard, perfect ridges of his abdomen. As I suspected, his entire torso was covered in the tattoos that wound up his neck and down his arms. The black, swirling glyphs were oddly elegant.

I reached out and touched his lean torso, surprised at

what I found. The tattoos helped cover the puckered slashes and jagged lines of scar tissue, but my fingers found the patches of hardened skin. They were everywhere.

Tears stung the back of my eyes. So much pain embedded in flesh.

He shoved me back, before taking several steps away. "What are you doing?" he asked in alarm.

"Wh-who did this to you?" I asked, closing my fingers into fists.

Before I knew what was happening, he grabbed his shirt and retreated to the other side of the room. Shucking it on, he didn't say a word as his face closed off.

"Tell me," I insisted, fighting against his instant shutdown.

"Believe me, princess, you don't want to know."

Then he threw open the French doors and disappeared.

I grabbed a robe and threw it on before rushing out onto the balcony. But he was gone.

Moments ago, I'd been desperate to have Gatsby inside me. Now, I was desperate to get inside him. Unravel the mystery of his past, where he'd been all these years, how he got those scars, and why he kept insisting he was the monster.

11

———

KAT

THE OVERWHELMING MIXTURE OF GATSBY'S PASSION, OFFSET by his sudden rejection, along with the words of those women at the party hammered into me without relief the rest of the night.

I still couldn't believe the things I let him do to me. I thought I knew myself, what I liked, what I would accept, but he'd turned me into some kind of animal. Smothering myself with my pillow, I tried to block out the memory of what he'd done and how badly I wanted it.

As much as I wanted to break out my "assistant" and fill the emptiness that still demanded satisfaction, I knew Gatsby wouldn't have gone far.

So instead, I slept like absolute shit, my sexual ache only burrowing in deeper into another kind of need. The need to be wrapped in someone's arms, to be told I'm safe, loved, and that everything would be okay.

I hadn't had that kind of love since my mother passed. My dad hadn't been much for physical affection, too much always on the move. His physical efforts went toward shaking hands and kissing babies. But right now, I wanted the security of a safe pair of arms. The permission that all I had to do was just be me.

To my surprise, a hot tear slid down my cheek. I wiped it away and pushed those feelings in a box.

I needed to get back to what was important, and that was being the respectable niece of a politician who was going to change the world. I had to close up my darkness and shame in a box to be the person I was supposed to. Family was about duty, and I knew how to fulfill those duties: support my family's political agenda, and don't embarrass them.

When the morning sun rays filled my room, my blood-shot eyes were already open to receive them. I dragged myself to the shower, the hot spray a brutal pressure against my unusually sensitive skin. But after emerging, I felt more like myself.

In the time it took to brush my teeth and lotion every inch of my skin, I scrounged up the strength to get through this day. I wasn't some shrinking violet who needed someone else to take care of her.

And more importantly, I had my first gallery showing tonight. Today would not be ruined by demons, doom, and a certain renegade angel who was likely sitting in my tree.

Throwing on a breezy summer dress that dipped low between my breasts, with cutouts on the side, I knew it would help beat the heat of the day. Then I slipped on some bright red sandals.

I pushed open my French doors and strode into the bright morning. The smell of fresh cut grass assailed me. It took me longer to find Gatsby in the tree than I thought it would. God, he was damned good at hiding in plain sight.

"Are you coming?" I asked Gatsby in an impatient tone. "There is a lot to do today."

If he insisted on being my shadow, we'd do it my way.

In a moment, he stood before me. All lean muscle, smelling like the fresh morning and something darker. Judging by the circles under his eyes, he hadn't slept much either.

Shooting him a flirty look from under my eyelashes, I noted how he instantly leaned an inch closer, his mouth parted.

"Do us both a favor and take a shower before you come down for breakfast." Then I turned and waltzed back into the house to go join my family in the dining room.

I could have sworn I heard a low growl behind me, and I ignored the shivers it sent racing up and down my spine.

My uncle John met me with a broad smile at the head of the table. "Don't you look summer-ready this morning?"

I allowed myself to follow the delicious smells of baked goods to the buffet table. I grabbed a plate and filled it up with eggs, fruit, and even plucked up a warm croissant. I needed something substantial to settle my tummy for the excitement of the day.

I smiled back, taking a seat across from Gabe. I caught sight of Dave through the windows. He was on the terrace, talking emphatically on his phone.

"Thank you, today's a big day." I poured a small glass of fresh-squeezed orange juice.

"It absolutely is." My uncle's smile broadened further. "Gabe," he prompted.

"Yes, congratulations," Gabe said, without looking up from his tablet.

"Well, I think congratulations are better saved until after tonight," I said, before tearing off some buttery croissant and popping it in my mouth.

A flash of confusion crossed my uncle's face. "Tonight…"

"You know," I said, "after people see my pieces in the gallery and don't immediately want to burn the place down."

My uncle gave a long blink as if trying to compute something.

"My gallery show, tonight?" I prompted. "That is what we were talking about, right?"

Gabe lifted his head finally to look over at me. "I thought you and Jimi got engaged."

I choked on my juice, some of it going up my nose with an acidic sting.

At that moment, Gatsby entered the room.

I worked to get control of my spasming throat.

In his same boots, jeans, and tight black tee shirt. The dark, defensive look on his face let me know he expected someone to protest his presence. Maybe he was used to being thrown out. He certainly lacked charm. I bet it happened more often than not.

The shock on my uncle's and cousin's face was overt. I didn't bring men to the breakfast table. In fact, my cousins didn't bring their flings to breakfast either. Not even Gabe's girlfriend, Molly, came to family breakfast. I wasn't even sure she'd ever slept over despite them being together for two years. Not that I'd slept with Gatsby or flung with him.

But the breakfast table was a family-only kind of deal, though no one had ever explicitly said so.

Able to speak again after the juice attack, I said, "This is Gatsby. He is my... assistant. He's going to help me get ready for the show tonight."

I didn't want to alarm my family that a demon might be after me and Gatsby was acting as bodyguard. I pointed at the table of food. "Help yourself."

With one more severe scan of the room, Gatsby walked over and grabbed a plate and immediately filled it with fresh bacon, sausage, a mountain of eggs, and then tried to balance a couple croissants on top.

His wet hair was a tousled mess, and when he sat down in the chair next to me, I inhaled his clean masculine scent and my mouth instantly watered. I crossed my legs under the table as moisture pooled elsewhere.

Dammit, Kat, you are at the family breakfast table. Keep it together.

But illicit flashes of last night heated my blood, even as I tried to think of something to cool me off.

Mud. Baseball. Law school.

That last one did the trick.

Gatsby dug into the food like a starving man. In the light of day, I was struck again by the fact I knew little to nothing about him. Where he was from, or how he'd defeated the She.

The way he ate, with such focus, reminded me of a cross between a starving child who didn't know when his next meal would come, and someone who served in the military. The thought caused a sharp pain in my heart.

My uncle and cousin watched Gatsby in stunned silence.

Dave finally strode back into the breakfast nook, having

ended his call. He stopped dead in his tracks, glaring at Gatsby. "Wasn't he at the party last night?"

"I invited him," I rushed to say. "We've been working nonstop on getting this gallery show ready. Plus, isn't it good to have another body of support at those functions?" I added with a hopeful smile to my uncle.

Gatsby's fork loudly scraped against the empty plate as he shoveled the last bite into his mouth. Once finished with the meal, he faced my uncle. "I heard you are up for reelection, sir. How is that going?" There was a steely gaze in Gatsby's eye as he spoke to my uncle.

Uncle John met it with a similar intensity. "Thank you for asking, young man. I believe yesterday's rally and last night's party put us back in the lead again."

"Glad to hear it," Gatsby said, not breaking eye contact.

What the hell kind of pissing match is this?

Dave was still standing, and Gabe's eyebrows practically reached his hairline. And that line had started receding in the last year.

"I didn't see your wife in attendance last night," Gatsby said.

I nudged him with my knee under the table, hoping to cue him away from the subject.

My uncle's lips thinned.

"My mother abandoned us when I was six," Dave said in a harsh tone meant to shut the subject down.

"Did she?" Gatsby asked, not looking away from my uncle. "I'm sorry to hear it."

My uncle looked down at his lap as he smoothed his napkin. The subject of my aunt always caused great pain, so we never spoke of her. Even the campaign was careful to highlight my uncle as an excellent single father and guardian of his niece in a way that didn't bring up his absentee wife.

I barely ate half my food, but the tension filling the room made my skin itch. With a loud clap of my hands, I said, "Well, lots to do. Let's get to it." Then to my uncle and cousins, I said with a hopeful smile, "I can't wait to see you all tonight."

They didn't utter a word as I grabbed Gatsby's arm and pulled him out of the room with me, toward the garage.

The instant we exited the dining room, Bear was there, clip-clopping alongside us, ready to be let out. Bear was typically shy with strangers, but he stuck to Gatsby's side even as Gatsby resolutely ignored my dog.

As soon as I opened the automatic door, Bear lumbered out, sniffing the grass until he did his business.

When it was time for him to go back in the house without us, he sat down on his fluffy butt and looked up at Gatsby.

"Bear," I said in warning. He turned to look at me, but then he went right back to staring at Gatsby.

I sighed and pinched the bridge of my nose.

"What?" he asked, clearly uncomfortable with the canine attention.

"Bear won't go in until you acknowledge him."

He frowned down at my dog. "Acknowledge?"

"You know, pet him? Pet the dog, and then he'll go in the house, and then we can get going."

Gatsby looked as though I asked him to chug straight lemon juice. But he reached out a hand and patted the top of my dog's head. Bear's tongue lolled out in a sign of encouragement.

Annoyance needled me. How could Gatsby seriously not

know how to pet a dog properly? But then I remembered the kittens I showed him, before they were all given away along with my mother's cat after my dad died.

What do you use them for?

Use them for? You love them.

Something in my heart pinched.

Before I could think too hard, I grabbed Gatsby's hand and smoothed it over Bear's head several times. "He also likes the back of his ears scratched."

A line formed between Gatsby's brows as he focused on scratching behind the dog's ears. Bear leaned into his touch, slobbering on Gatsby's pants. Then satisfied, Bear trotted back inside.

Finally, we could get on our way. A car was a much better idea, since I wasn't ready to get back on a bike, especially not with Gatsby's hard body pressed against my backside.

After I buckled in, I paused before starting the car, feeling Gatsby's eyes burning a hole in my side. That clean masculine scent filled the car, an inescapable, heady concoction.

"About last night," he said slowly. His eyes dropped to my lips as if he were going to kiss me again, and I found myself holding my breath.

Then he shifted and looked at the dashboard. "It was a mistake."

My hands found the smooth leather of the steering wheel, and I tried to ground myself there. "Couldn't have said it better myself."

"It won't happen again," he said, his voice low and gravelly. His presence in the car pressing on me like a physical weight I wanted to succumb to.

My finger punched the garage button, and then I turned the ignition. "Absolutely not."

"Good."

"Great," I said.

Gatsby accompanied me to the radio station where I had a seven-minute interview to spotlight the gallery show. After that, we went to my favorite coffee shop.

I collapsed onto my favorite red plush couch, forcing Gatsby to sit next to me. The massive mug they gave me was close to overflowing with the hot white froth of my cappuccino. I opened my laptop and got to work.

Invisible pressure pressed against me. I tried to ignore it, but I barely managed five minutes before I looked up.

"What are you doing?" I asked.

"Nothing," Gatsby said.

"Not nothing, you're staring at me," I countered, my fingers sliding across the keys, the pads of my fingertips outlining the square buttons without pressing them. Gatsby's gaze continued to press heavily against me, heating up my skin. It made me want to cross the mere inches between us and thread my fingers between his strong, warm ones.

I hated that.

"I'm protecting you," he countered.

"Can't you read a book or something? And protect me while doing your own thing?"

A buzzing sound interrupted. At first, I'd thought it was one of the espresso machines, but the sound built into a cacophony. Looking out the front window, I caught sight of a black mass of what appeared to be bugs. They descended on a man walking by. His screams pierced through the glass, until the meat all but disappeared. He collapsed to the ground.

My mouth turned to sandpaper as my stomach dropped.

One minute he was a perfectly normal guy, the next, he was no more than a heap of picked-over bones. It all happened so fast.

But the buzzing mass didn't stop there. It smacked into the large front window of the coffee shop. My eyes rounded as I took in the creatures up close. They weren't bugs at all. They were tiny pixies, with wings like a dragonfly's, wide mouths full of razor-sharp teeth, and beady, malevolent eyes. Their arms and wings beat at the glass. A crackle hailed a number of hairline fractures in glass as the pixies continually rammed into it.

Gatsby jumped up and bellowed. "Everyone take cover."

My mind raced so fast I couldn't grasp any one thought. Gatsby grabbed me and pushed me to the floor, then he picked up the couch we'd been sitting on. He flipped it over and dropped it on top of me. For a second, I feared being squished, but only the weight of the cushions pressed down on me.

The front window shattered, and the buzzing grew as loud as a chainsaw.

A gap in the cushions allowed me to see Gatsby face off against the buzzing cloud. He threw a hand up and light emerged from it, forcing the mass to hold in place. His jaw clenched, and his muscles shook as he tried to keep the dark force at bay. A racket of tables flipping, heavy footfalls, and screams and gasps mixed in the background. The buzzing grew louder, drowning out the cacophony of panicking coffee shop patrons.

Fear and awe fought for dominance as I watched Gatsby use a power I'd seen twice before. Once when Gatsby had driven off the demon in my father's study. The second time had been on television from a helicopter news camera during a massive battle of good vs evil in the streets of downtown Denver. A group of men had used their powers to subdue a woman who controlled the forces of darkness. Had Gatsby been one of them? How did he have his powers? Had he been one of those people I'd seen on television that day?

It wasn't long before Gatsby's arm shook harder as the light he emitted flickered. He cried out as if in pain, and the sound grew louder until he was yelling what sounded like a war cry.

Whatever force he was harnessing, he was losing it. He wouldn't last much longer, which meant the dark pixies would pick him dry of his flesh the moment he gave out. And his sword, which lay on the ground now, wouldn't do any good against the miniature horde. My mind scrambled. I needed to do something, but there was nothing I could think of.

Gatsby fell to his knees, shaking like a leaf now, the light barely holding.

He was going to die, trying to save everyone in here. My heart leapt up into my throat as I worked to bring clarity to my panicked thoughts.

An idea struck. I fought my way out from under the couch.

"Kat, no," Gatsby bellowed, fear flashing hot and bright in his eyes.

I raced to the back of the coffee shop and jumped over the counter to grab the cannister I hoped would be there. I ran back to Gatsby with it in hand, pulling the pin in a fluid movement before hitting the trigger.

I sprayed the flesh-eating pixies with the fire extinguisher. The white spray took the pixies down in sticky globs, just as Gatsby's light went out and he fell hard on his side with a grunt. The pixies were all contained on the floor now. They struggled in the white goo, so I ran over and began stomping them. Tiny shrill screams filled the air as I continued to bring my sandals down over and over, smashing their tiny evil bodies.

"Whoa, whoa, chill out," a woman's voice cut through my consciousness. "You can stop now."

I hadn't realized I'd been screaming in rage, until she yelled over me. I looked up and met the dark wide eyes of a pale woman with black hair and Bettie Page bangs. She wore deliberately tattered punk-rock clothes and big boots.

A few steps behind her stood a slim, tall man with sandy blond hair and green eyes. He wore a Metallica T-shirt and the same gear as the woman. They both held wands that were hooked up to their large backpacks—like punk Ghostbusters.

"Take a step back," the woman directed me.

A couple tiny arms and wings still fluttered in the extinguisher foam. The dark-haired woman pointed the wand in her hand at them and hit a trigger. Fire cascaded from the wand, engulfing the remaining pixies. Shrill screams rose into the air. She didn't stop until they were silenced. Then the man came over with a blanket and threw it over the flames, putting them out.

I ran to Gatsby, who was coming to. I helped him up into a sitting position. His taut arm muscles flexed under my hands, sending an electric jolt through my belly. My mouth tasted bitter, a side effect of the terror that struck me when he collapsed. I still didn't know if he was my savior or my bane, but I needed him to be okay.

All the coffee shop patrons ran out in a hurry, not even bothering to see if we were alright. I couldn't blame them. We lived in a terrifying new reality. Everyone was trying to survive with their sanity.

"Cripes, is this how you destroyed that demon girl?" I asked, realizing I was panting. I wasn't sure if it was from the running or the adrenaline.

"No," Gatsby rasped. "Chopping off her head worked just fine."

I helped him to his feet, so that his warmth and weight pressed against me. I instantly had the thought I never wanted to let him go.

"Holy twinkies, is that you, Gatsby?" The lanky man asked.

Gatsby's expression darkened.

"Shit," the girl exclaimed with a laugh of disbelief. "If you or this chick hadn't acted fast, everyone in here would be a pile of bones."

"You know these people?" I asked Gatsby, still enjoying the feel of his body. He didn't move away either.

It was then I noticed a black van parked in the middle of the road behind the man. "Whack A Ghoul," I said, reading the big, blocky neon letters.

"At your service." The girl tipped an invisible hat. "I'm Krystan, and that hot stud behind me is Travis."

A Jeep screeched to a stop next to the van. A blonde woman hopped out of the driver's side. The door behind the driver's seat swung open as a guy well over six and a half feet with a beard and long hair stepped out too. He reminded me of a Viking. Then from around the other side of the car came another tall beefcake with impossibly blue eyes and dark hair. I couldn't decide if he reminded me more of Superman or Clark Kent.

The beefcake's eyes widened when he spotted the man leaning against me. "Gatsby."

Instantly, Gatsby pushed me away. His face tightened and shoulders tensed. "Calan."

"Gatsby," the Viking boomed in friendly greeting, either not noticing, or ignoring the icy vibes coming off Gatsby.

The blonde made her way to Krystan but cast a wary eye in Gatsby's direction.

"You are out, fighting the good fight," the Viking continued in a cheerful tone. "You have changed your mind and wish to join forces again? We could lay waste to—"

"I didn't stop them, Leonidas," Gatsby snapped. He jerked his head toward me. "She did."

All eyes turned toward me. I was used to public scrutiny, so I instantly rolled my shoulders back, and lifted my chin in an easy smile that didn't reach my eyes.

"Well done," the blonde woman said, shooting me a friendly smile. "It isn't an easy feat to take down a swarm."

"Emma's right," Krystan snorted, referring to the blonde. "I'd rather fight a demon dog or a crib any day over a fucking swarm of itty-bitty biters."

Though something was very off in the air between these people, especially the man named Calan and Gatsby, something in me instinctually wanted to like the two women.

"Gatsby, how have you been?" Calan asked. His blue eyes radiated sincere concern.

Gatsby refused to meet them, instead staring beyond Calan, as if he were inconsequential. "Alone, which is how I like it."

"It doesn't have to be that way," Calan said.

"Didn't you hear me, Calan?" Gatsby said. "I said that's how I like it."

The Viking man's face fell, as if disappointed in Gatsby's answer.

"Is that why you tattooed yourself in sigils?" Emma asked, as she looked over Gatsby's arms and up his neck. A sadness tinged her words. "So we couldn't find you?"

"That's smart," Calan commented.

"I don't need your approval," Gatsby snapped. "I never have, never will."

Calan frowned. "Of course you don't."

"You think you are different than our masters, Calan? Now that you run the five orders, maybe you are simply turning into them."

"That's not true," Emma protested. "There are no more lies, no more manipulations. Everyone works together to fight the Stygian." She walked over to Calan and slipped her hand into his. "Everyone has freedom now. To do what they want and be with who they want." She shot a meaningful look at me.

I shifted my weight under her gaze, suddenly uncomfortable.

Gatsby's tone turned vicious. "The girl is business. As in *my* business, not yours, is that clear?"

The sting of rejection and the warmth of his possessiveness mingled into an incomprehensible feeling that left me on the cusp of everything and nothing. I wasn't sure if I liked it or not, but either way I felt the sudden and deep desire to process those feelings in private.

"Grab your things," Gatsby commanded to me in a low tone, as he picked up his sword. I didn't hesitate. I grabbed my upturned laptop, shoving it in my bag. As soon as I'd done so, Gatsby grabbed my arm.

"Looks like you got the cleanup well in hand," Gatsby

said to the people standing around, leading us out toward the door.

We had to pass Calan to get to my car. He stopped Gatsby with a hand on the shoulder.

"We could use good men like you," Calan said. Pain, maybe guilt, flashed in his eyes.

Gatsby shrugged him off. "I'm not looking to be used anymore, and I'm sure as hell not good."

12

GATSBY

"So what's the deal with Mickey Blue Eyes?" Kat asked as she drove us away. I didn't bother looking to see if Calan watched us leave. And I didn't bother asking where we were going.

"What?"

Kat recoiled. I realized my voice came out sharper than I meant it too. I was still on edge from the run-in, but she didn't deserve that.

"What is a mickey blue eyes?" I asked. It was frustrating when I didn't get people's references or slang, which was often. It reminded me of my upbringing.

"I mean," she said in a quiet voice, "who was the guy

with blue eyes? His name was Calan?"

"He's... my brother," I said after a moment.

"Wow, you look nothing alike."

"Leonidas is also my brother. But none of us are biologically related," I said, hearing the defensiveness creep back into my tone.

"Then how are you brothers?" Kat asked, shooting me a side-eyed glance.

I didn't talk about this. Not to anybody, not ever.

"We are... were Knights of the Light. We were taken at birth, the chosen ones, and raised in a temple well hidden from civilization by a secret cult known as the Order of Luxis. From the beginning, we were trained to be soldiers, warriors to fight the darkness of the Stygian, the hell dimension that opened up and spilled over onto ours. For hundreds of years, our dimensions have brushed against each other, and darkness has come onto our lands, and it is the Chevalier's duty to hunt it down and destroy it. Until last year, it had remained a secret from civilization. But now the world knows that demons and evil spirits exist."

A deep line formed between her eyebrows. "And you've been fighting these things since you were how old?"

She turned the car onto the familiar route I'd learned led to the art studio.

"Since the beginning. I was one of the lucky five to survive the trials, along with Calan and Leonidas. They sent us into the jungles and set magic-made beasts on us. If we survived the trials and emerged from the jungle, we would be named the true Knights of the Light."

A bitter taste filled my mouth as it always did when I thought of the trials. I'd emerged from the jungle poisoned, delirious, with broken bones and deep wounds. When the remaining few of us stood over the bodies of our fallen brothers, I couldn't help the tears that spilled from my eyes. I was the only one who mourned for our fallen brethren. Calan stood stone-faced, as if they were strangers laid out before us, and was commended for his poise.

Master Wu punished me after, for my weakness. Anytime I felt even the barest prickle of tears in my eyes, my back would light with phantom fire. My flesh remembers the wrath of my master's switch. He'd beaten all the tears out of me, leaving only anger behind.

"Wow, a knight," she breathed. "Like King Arthur and—"

"No," I cut her off. "Those were tales of heroes. We were knights, but we were considered damned. Our masters lied to and manipulated us into perfect obedience. I was considered the weakest of the order. My magic was flawed and unreliable. And no matter how many lessons they gave me, I did not improve."

"Lessons?" she asked.

A dark grin curled my lips. "Beatings, weeks without food, endless hours of physical training. Anything they could think of to train me into a better soldier. My master threw his all into schooling me. Of all my brothers, I believe I had the most cruel, sadistic master."

Kat had felt the scars. The pity I saw on her face left a scar bigger than any of those on my body. I didn't deserve pity. Kat should run me right through with a knife and never look back.

Again, that woman's brown eyes appeared in my mind, right as her life was extinguished by my sword. Did her children wish to seek vengeance against me? Would I meet one of them in a couple years in a dark alleyway where they would slip a knife in my gut? Would I even bother to stop them?

"Where is this bastard now?" Kat asked, referring to my master. Her voice was tight, as her knuckles shifted where she gripped the wheel.

"Dead," I said, flatly.

The voice of Master Wu spoke up in my mind. *But you can never get rid of me, can you, lemon?*

"Good." Kat raised her chin. "Or I would have found him and laid some serious hurt on the guy. But if you all grew up together in this... Order of Luxis, why aren't you buddy-buddy with the only other people who went through the same thing as you?"

She'd brought it back around to Calan.

"Calan was my superior in every way. He was the good son who always did what was asked of him and executed it with perfection and obedience. That is, until he met Emma. Then he revolted against our masters to save her. The world almost ended because of their love. A couple of times, actually."

"That doesn't answer my question," Kat said in a careful tone.

A humorless laugh escaped me. "Because. For every challenge he overcame, I was punished for my failings. The more prodigious his accomplishments, the more powerful his magic, the more I was punished for not being like him. He was the good son, and I was the bad son. The stain of my existence only lent to the brightness of his light."

"But that's not his fault... is it?"

"He didn't care. He was too busy being the perfect son to notice how it lent to my suffering." It wasn't until I finished that I realized I'd been yelling.

The echo of my words rang out like a physical buzz in the small car space. I expected Kat to recoil, to call me a monster, a selfish, stupid child.

Instead, she chewed on her bottom lip as if deep in thought, and then said, "So you don't know why your powers don't work as reliably as your brothers'?"

"It wasn't until much later that we discovered our magic comes from a single unbreakable belief. The order had meant to make us believe our sole existence was to destroy the darkness to repent for our lost souls."

"You don't believe you were meant to repent?" she asked. "I'm not saying you ever truly needed to, but that is some serious cult-level brainwashing. And if you didn't fall for their story, what is the belief that gives you the powers you have now? I mean, they aren't reliable, but you still have them, right? So, you must have some idea of what fuels it."

"If I knew that, don't you think I would have figured it out and fixed the problem by now?" I snapped.

"Right," she said, pulling up to the studio and throwing the car into park.

Then she turned toward me. "I know it's none of my business, but blood or not, those guys are your family, and it seems like you could have a place with them, if you wanted."

I leaned in, a snarl plastered on my lips so she wouldn't misunderstand me. "I don't want it. I meant what I said, I prefer to be alone." I gestured to my tattoos. "They are sigils, so no one can track me with their magic. I've worked very hard to be alone."

Kat's tone turned icy. "Well, it's a good thing I'm just business, then."

"Isn't it just?"

We sat there, locked in a stare. I couldn't tell if we were fighting or in vehement agreement. All I knew was she made my blood boil. And that was dangerous. I practically jumped out of the car and rounded it to jerk her door open. Kat stepped out and gave me one more cool glare before grabbing her bag and leading the way to the coffee shop below the studio.

Kat stopped to grab another cappuccino, since hers had been ruined in the melee. As we ascended the stairs to the studio, a buzz of activity could be heard from inside. Kat shot me a look. I gently pushed my way past her. I grabbed the hilt of my sword, pulling it from my sheath, and opened the door to the studio, ready for whatever was on the other side.

But absolutely nothing could have prepared me for this.

The teachers and students were exclaiming in excitement over the pieces of art set on display.

"The use of color is absolutely masterful. Do you see the way she uses the warm colors of light that reach out to the boy, stuck in darkness?"

"The way his eyes peer out from the tree, how did she manage to capture such intensity? It's positively memorizing."

I couldn't move, couldn't breathe.

Kat pushed her way past me, only to be stopped short with a strangled gasp of horror. The cup clacked against the wood floor, froth and coffee splattering all over for the second time.

Then her wild eyes turned toward me, with the fearful expression of a cornered animal.

All of the paintings were of me as a boy. There must have been thirty of them. Of me hovering over a cup of hot chocolate, intense curiosity with a hint of a smile at the corner of my mouth. I could almost smell the cocoa, feel the warmth coming off the mug in the picture.

Of me hiding in the tree outside her balcony in the dead of night. I stared out from the branches, my eyes glittering like hard diamonds that could cut through anything.

I found myself drawn in by one of me curled in on myself in a dark room, my head down, not noticing the streaks of light reaching out toward me. The cold blues and grays that surrounded me kept me trapped and blinded. But those rays, they were coming for me whether I knew it or not, and the movement of the paint communicated they couldn't be stopped.

"Wh-what the hell?" Kat sputtered.

The curvy girl with heavy eyeliner, who I'd learned was her friend, but didn't know her name, trotted up, her hands flapping nervously. Her words tripped over each other. "I'm so sorry, Kat. The gallery curator came and said she was here to pick up the last couple pieces for the show. We couldn't find them, and while I was searching, she got Sam to open your private closet to see if they were in there. Please don't be mad, Sam thought he was helping."

"And he was helping," a woman's voice interrupted. She approached, wearing white overalls, cat-eye glasses connected by a sparkly chain, and a fancy hair updo. I recognized her as the woman who ran the gallery where Kat's show was supposed to be. They'd had several meetings in the previous weeks that I'd watched from the shadows.

"The pieces you gave me were good, Kat, but these..." The curator opened a hand at the mini show behind her. "These are tremendous, moving, striking. And you had them locked up?"

My eyes connected with a piece unlike the rest. Unable to help myself, I moved toward it. It was done more recently than the others. I could smell the paint fumes more strongly, and instead of the visage of a boy, she'd created the face of a man.

My face.

She must have done it the day after I'd saved her from

the She. I'd followed her, of course, watching from the building next door as she furiously painted.

Half of it still needed detailing, but my eyes were finished. She used the same colors as the painting of me as a boy in a dark corner. I'd been recreated in blues, blacks, and grays, but this time, the warm, unstoppable light was in my eyes. As if a powerful magic were barely being kept at bay inside me.

The curator went on. "Kat, we need these pieces. You said you want to do this thing for real? This is how we do it. Admittedly, I wasn't entirely unmotivated to give you a show because of who your uncle is, but honey—"

Out of my periphery, I could see her take Kat's hands in hers. "You let me show these and the only name we will need is yours."

One of the male students who stood nearby in a small cluster took notice of me. "Hey, you look just like..." His voice died as he realized.

Kat pulled her hands away from the curator and spoke in an unnaturally loud voice. "The remaining paintings for the show were left downstairs with the barista. I left a message with your assistant. I had these locked up for a reason, and no one had a right to open that door without my permission, much less drag them out for everyone to see."

A burly man with a ponytail and beard, wearing a flannel plaid shirt, stepped forward. "Kat, I'm so sorry, I didn't mean—"

The curator raised her hand. "Don't apologize, Mr. Rutgar. These were too good to be kept hidden away, that is the magic of the world. It will always reveal what is necessary. But I understand, Kat, you need time to come to terms."

"Could everyone please leave?" Kat demanded, in that

unnatural voice again. She seemed on the verge of screaming, breaking down, or running. But I couldn't help her.

What I felt was so overwhelming I almost couldn't control it. It bubbled and pushed its way up even though I wanted to stay calm and collected.

"Yes, of course," Sam said, before ushering everyone out.

I finally tore my gaze away from the painting, having seen more than enough.

The curator grabbed Kat's shoulders. "Don't let fear stand in your way. It is the only true gatekeeper between you and your dreams."

Then she left, along with Kat's friend, who seemed reluctant to go. Still, she shut the door behind her, leaving only Kat and me surrounded by her paintings.

"I... I never meant for you to see these." Kat stuttered almost uncontrollably. She pinched and wrung either hand. I'd seen Kat face a She demon and a swarm of flesh-eating pixies, but right now, she looked far more terrified having to face me.

"How many years have you been—" I swept an arm toward the pictures when I couldn't finish. My voice was gruff, as what felt like a stormy ocean thrashed about inside me.

Her hands dropped as if she were defeated. "The very next day after you left." She took a step toward the one with me balled up in a dark corner. "I started in pencil and charcoals. I wasn't very good, but it was the only thing that kept me from crying. The only thing that made me feel sane. Drawing made me feel like you were still... with me. I drew more and more, then moved on to paintings, and made so many pictures of you standing between me and that... thing. The nurses at the institution said it wasn't healthy. They said I had to let go of the nightmare and a made-up boy."

My hands fisted. I tried to swallow, but a lump caught in my throat.

"I was so scared and alone, I drew more and more until they took my art supplies away. But I'd still trace pictures of you on the floor, on the walls, on the sheets."

Kat's hands visibly shook as she wiped away the tears falling from her eyes.

"I learned to stop talking about the demon, and they thought I stopped drawing you. But I kept drawing you in my palm to keep you close, until my uncle pulled me out." She went on, her voice getting louder as her fists clenched. "They had no right. No right at all to pull these out. They were mine, and they were private. And I never meant for anyone to see them, least of all you."

We fell into a long silence.

A half hiccup, half sob emerged from her. "Say something. My feelings are literally splattered all over this room. Please say something. What are you feeling?" Her arms crossed over her stomach.

"I don't know how to feel," I started, then stopped. "No, that's not right. I feel... exposed." My voice came out low, dangerous.

She sucked in a breath on a hiss as if she were in pain, but I didn't let that stop me. She wanted to know how I felt? She'd have to take the brunt of it all now.

"You realize that all these years, I have never let a single person catch me on camera. And here you are, painting dozens of pictures of me." As my voice grew louder, her arms tightened farther over her stomach.

I never felt so much as when I was with her. Anger and resentment rotted in me every day, but the things she made me feel... Like there was more than that, like she could see to my innermost pain, to my innermost desire, and in the final painting of me as a man, to my innermost strength. I couldn't put words to the embarrassment, the raw, primal need I suddenly felt to be the man in that picture she created.

I didn't want to feel any of this. I wanted things to stay the way they were. Emotion and feeling crashed over me like unforgiving waves of the ocean until I wasn't sure who I was or what I would do anymore.

"I feel stupid." My voice boomed through the room with anger now. "Stupid for thinking of you all these years, knowing you probably despised me. But the way you paint me here, like I'm something you want to save."

"You aren't something to be saved, you are someone to be lov—" Kat tried to stop herself before she finished.

In a second, I was in front of her, my hand around her throat, squeezing with enough pressure that she could still breathe but couldn't speak another word. "Don't say that. Don't you ever say that. You don't know what I am."

Her eyes moved past me in a deliberate motion. I followed them to the picture of me curled up in the darkness. It was next to the one of me as a man. The light sparked bright and hot in my eyes.

Suddenly I was swept away, my anger gone with it.

Then I turned back to face her. She looked resigned to her fate, as if she expected me to break her neck for what she had done.

I released my hold on her throat. A horrid confession I tried to kill and bury fought its way up. My fingers tunneled in her hair as I looked down at her impossibly beautiful fucking face. "I kept you close too."

Then I leaned down and kissed her.

13

KAT

GATSBY KISSED ME SO GENTLY, SO DEEPLY, A FIRE STARTED AT my toes and slowly but thoroughly consumed me.

It was different than the last time. In the dead of night, he'd tried to punish me, shock me. Now a message imprinted from his lips onto mine over and over again.

Thank you. Thank you. Thank you.

A dam of need broke in me. In a minute, I had his shirt off. I sighed in relief when I touched his bare flesh. My hands traveled over the scarred, tattooed surface of his hard, lean muscle.

My shirt disappeared, and then my bra. Gatsby gathered

me close, pressing my bare chest against his and a sob of emotion caught in my chest but didn't go any higher.

He continued to kiss me like I was his salvation. Someone to be worshipped, protected at all costs. We stripped the rest of the way, and my eyes widened as I saw what he'd not been so subtly hiding in his pants. His hand wrapped around his long, thick shaft. A bead of precum glistened at the tip, making my mouth water.

For a split second I worried he wouldn't fit, but that thought was instantly chased away by the anticipation of being filled until I couldn't think a single fucking thought.

I needed him. I needed him like air. Like I hadn't taken a breath since that day he left me.

My hand pushed his aside to grasp his rigid length. I reveled in stroking him, his cock like steel wrapped in velvet. His hands tightened in my hair as his face screwed up like I was killing him. He was completely at my mercy.

Then he pushed me away before pulling my hand, leading me up the three short steps of the dais at the center of the room. It was where the models usually posed for classes. Gatsby sat me down, then knelt before me at the bottom step. The cheap carpet scratched against my sensitive skin, heightening the reality that this was happening.

Gatsby's elbows spread my legs apart, and they easily opened. "I have to taste you. If I don't, I might die," he confessed.

With a final dark look of promise and passion, he dipped down and licked me from bottom to top. My head fell back as my fingers tangled in his hair. His slick tongue was everywhere at once, sucking, licking, playing, and when his fingers joined the party, I no longer knew where I was as my hips bucked wildly under him. Only the faint smell of acrylics and clay reminded me I was still on Earth. Every other part of me had been jettisoned to another height.

The pressure started deep at my center and built steadily toward a precipice I'd never reached before. Breathing was no longer an option and my vision turned fuzzy.

Pressing his digits into me, stretching me, heat engulfed every inch of me. He pumped with vigor, pushing my already unsteady emotions to the edge of climax. Strange, wanton sounds came out of my throat as I neared completion.

Gatsby suddenly stopped, retreating from my body. I could have cried, my frustration turned sharp as my inner muscles clenched and pulsated with a painful need.

Then he was there, pushing me onto my back, sliding his body over mine, looking at me with such feeling it caused my gut to clench.

As the tip of his hardness brushed against my greedy opening, Gatsby seemed to have to almost force his words out. "You make me feel like I'm... more. Like I could be the man you think I am."

"What did you do that was so bad?"

"Shh," he hushed me, closing his eyes tight. "For this one time, I'm going to let myself forget the bastard I am. In this moment, I'm the man you want me to be. The one in those paintings. Then later I can go back to being the monster I truly am."

Before I could protest, he pushed inside of me. My knees drew up as I worked to take him. Pain and pleasure battled as he stretched me. But as soon as he was inside, he began a steady thrust and brought me back to the edge of my pleasure.

Even as his hips found a steady rhythm, a hand smoothed the hair back from my face.

"Fuck, princess. I never believed in heaven until I met you."

I had fallen for a figment of my imagination. Everyone had told me I was crazy. but now my imagination had been turned into flesh once again. And he was here, making love to me with a passionate abandon that exceeded any dream I'd had.

My hands clawed at his back, as if I could make him more real. As if I could keep him from slipping away, even though I knew we were on borrowed time.

Suddenly, all those nights in the institution when I was eleven, with no one but the ghost of a boy with no name to keep me company, were worth it. And with Gatsby pushing into me, covering me, I felt whole for the first time since that week I met him.

His deep thrusts grew more frantic, and a hot fuzz overtook my brain. I never wanted to think again if it meant holding onto this feeling.

Gatsby's face screwed up and I could tell he was about to come. The very thought sent me hurtling over my own peak. My back lifted off the scratchy carpet as I pressed into him. Our sweaty bodies strained against each other in unison while a flood of heat filled me. My thighs quivered as shoots of pleasure rocketed through me.

A brief panic flitted through my mind as I realized we hadn't used a condom. Gatsby made me reckless beyond all measure. But the pleasure of my continuing orgasm washed away my senses.

"That's my princess," he hummed into my ear as I came down from the high.

In post-coital bliss, I looked up into the eyes of the man

who haunted my dreams for over a decade. They held such yearning, such pain, and pure devotion.

He loves you.

I caught the thought in my hand, as soon as it appeared, closing my fingers tightly around it. He'd never say it. He'd never stay. I couldn't break myself on words he never uttered. I buried that thought in the ground next to all my other dreams.

A line drew between his eyebrows. As if Gatsby could sense my sudden sadness.

With a reassuring half smile, I swallowed over the lump in my throat and pushed away the hair that fell in his eyes.

Footfalls on the steps up to the studio shattered the moment. It was time to return to reality before someone found us.

And there were mere hours left before my gallery show. I wondered how many life-changing things could happen in one day?

GATSBY

THE GALLERY SHOW WAS IN FULL SWING. BACK IN MY ILL-fitting suit, I made sure to stick to the background, where I could watch. Kat was glorious in her gold dress and high heels. It made her bronze skin glow as if she'd been transformed into some kind of goddess. I knew it wasn't the dress, though.

It was her art. When she spoke about it, when she painted, Kat lit up with a visible glow of pleasure. It magnetized everyone to her, and I told myself it was enough to feel the edges of that warmth from where I stood.

After we'd cleaned up and dressed quickly in the studio, though I didn't give a damn who walked in on us, Kat remained firm that the pictures were to go back into the closet. Though she paused by the one of me huddled in the corner as a boy, her fingers playing with the edge of the canvas.

The pain in that painting was so private, so close to me. But I nodded at her, giving her silent permission to add it to the show.

Kat deserved to shine, and my pain was inconsequential. I would have cut out my own heart and handed it to her on the spot if she asked.

No matter how big the crowd got, her eyes kept finding me. A mixture of sensual memory mixed with a pure unadulterated joy shone from them. She was in her element. These people saw her for what she was, but I could tell she wanted to remain connected to me. The selfish part of me absolutely preened at the knowledge.

Mine, mine, mine.

I shouldn't think such things. They would only be the memories I would cut myself on later.

Eventually, the crowd gave her a break and Kat's friend, Viet, joined her.

We'd officially met at the beginning of the show. She didn't ask questions even though I saw them crowded behind her dark eyes. I appreciated that.

The two women didn't notice I was close enough to hear them, as I pretended to be absorbed in a painting. I'd already memorized all the lines of her pictures, so I could save them for later in my mind when I was alone, stuck in a world of gray again.

"They shouldn't have done that," Viet said quietly. "Pulled your art out from the closet before you were ready. I tried to stop them, but I should have tried harder."

Kat sighed. "No, Viet, it's not your fault."

Anger tinged the other woman's voice now. "They literally dragged you out from the closet. The curator said you needed to come to terms with bringing it out in the open, but that is nonsense. Art is so personal. It's your joy, your pain. You should get to choose the time and place you want to share it, if at all. If that happened to me, I would have freaked out."

"You mean like how I did?" Kat said, smiling around her glass of champagne.

"Worse." Viet gave a solemn nod. "Nancy may have an impeccable eye for art, but she is no artist." Viet suddenly grabbed Kat's hand, looking up at her with feeling. "Everyone can't stop talking about 'the boy in darkness,' but I hope you did it for you. And I want you to know if you do need a place to share your joy, your pain, outside or inside your art, I'm here. I care about you. I hope you feel that."

I watched Kat's reaction. She seemed taken aback and an unnamed fear flitted across her eyes before she was back to normal. "Of course, Viet. I know that."

"You can trust me," Viet went on. "I know you are surrounded by these hoity-toity types who care more about your uncle's campaign or whatever the fuck, but I'm here for you. Whenever you want it or need it."

Kat looked at the champagne glass in her hand as she rolled the stem between her fingers. Her eyes had turned misty.

"Thank you, Viet." She squeezed her friend's hand back.

Despite her thanks, I knew that look in Kat's eyes. She stood behind a glass wall, and as much as she wanted to trust Viet, she couldn't let herself. Kat was surrounded by people who wanted things—they tore and grasped for purchase on power and money. It went beyond what people sought to get from her relationship to her uncle, who was a powerful man. Those people didn't see Kat for what she was. I heard the whispers at the parties. She was rich, privileged, and beautiful, so she deserved to suffer the most. To have everything ripped from her perfect fingers and ground in the dirt, so she would know pain.

No one saw the pain she carried. How she tried to squeeze herself into a box, rearranging her bones to fit a shape that wasn't her own. All to secure a modicum of love and respect from her family. How acutely lonely she was in the sea of vapid, insatiable predators that nibbled on caviar and sipped thousand-dollar champagne.

The two women were interrupted by patrons walking up to talk to Kat about her work. I took a moment to study Viet. She was good and true.

I should know. I'd been surrounded by those qualities my whole life; told I should become them though I couldn't. I may not be good, but I certainly had learned to identify what I was not.

And Kat needed someone like that in her life.

Especially after I was gone.

A couple caught my attention. They held hands and whispered sweet nothings into each other's ears. Even as friends joined them, they didn't break away.

An image of me standing next to Kat, my hand on her lower back as she chatted with her fans, struck me. As soon as I envisioned it, I shook it off. That wasn't my life. That wasn't me. I stayed back, watching and waiting.

For the next half hour as the party began to die down, Kat's head swiveled back and forth. Anxiety tightened the edges of her eyes, as they bounced to the door continually. I knew who she was waiting for, and I could offer no comfort in the matter. Her family had yet to show up.

Viet threw her arms around Kat one last time. "Are you going to meet us for drinks afterward?

"I hope so, but I'm a bit worn out," Kat said, sounding weary. "We'll see."

"Okay, a bunch of us will be at the club, Syn, going on about your success. I hope you'll come." Then with a final hug, she left. Viet paused when she passed the older man who entered. She sent a hopeful smile back at Kat and shot her two thumbs up.

The man who arrived was Kat's uncle.

Kat rolled her shoulders back and straightened, a hopeful smile blossoming on her face as her uncle approached. I drew back, deeper into the shadows, so he wouldn't notice me.

"You came," she said.

"Yes, your cousins couldn't make it, but of course, I wanted to see how you've been spending your time."

Kat hugged her uncle, and he gave her a gentle pat on the back. The look in his eyes told me he was anything but thrilled to be here. But when he pulled back, he gave her a tight-lipped smile.

There were only a few people left milling around, so Kat trailed next to her uncle as he walked from painting to painting, giving each a silent assessment. His expression remained neutral, not giving anything away. Kat's eyes were glued to his face, trying to gauge his reaction as she wrung her hands.

Finally, they came to stop before the painting of me.

"Is this..." He trailed off.

"The boy I spoke about as a kid? Yes," she said, suddenly very still.

He stepped in closer to her and said something I

couldn't hear. Both expression and color drained from her face.

When he backed up, her Uncle John said, "I'm glad you've enjoyed your little holiday, and these paintings are cute—"

"Cute," Kat echoed.

"—but this is where it stops, Katherine."

Kat folded her hands in front of her, her head dropping.

My fists clenched at my side. I could see him visibly destroying her dreams.

Uncle John lifted her chin with a knuckle. He let out a heavy sigh. "There, there. You are a good girl, and you know the right thing to do. We must sacrifice in our family for the greater good. It is our lot. But that is what ties us together."

It took every ounce of my control not to fly at the man and crack his neck.

Her uncle dropped his hand. "Tomorrow we will announce your intention to attend law school so we can celebrate at your birthday party on Saturday." Then in a softer voice, he added, "Cheer up, Katherine. The election is going well, and we all have a bright future before us."

With that, he walked past her and out of the gallery. Kat continued to stare forward as if she gazed directly into the Stygian itself. Her arms hung limp at her sides, and the terrible emptiness in her eyes inspired the most incomparable rage I'd ever known.

In a moment, I stood before her. She stared right through me. "Kat. Don't listen to him. You are in control of your future."

She didn't move, didn't blink, still caught in whatever hell churned in her mind's eye. So I took her by the shoulders and gave her a slight shake.

"You don't owe him anything. This is your life. You should be free to live it how you want."

Finally, her eyes focused on me. But instead of the usual warmth I found there, they were dark and defensive. "You don't understand." She turned to walk away, but I grabbed her wrist and pulled her back to me.

"I don't understand? I was born into a brainwashing cult, determined to use me. I had no say in my present or my future. But I got out. I am free. You can be free too."

Her eyebrows furrowed as she tried to get me to release her wrist, but I refused to let go. "It's not as easy for me."

My grip released at that, her hand slipping away.

"Easy." A sound of disbelief emerged from my throat. "You think I had it easy?"

"They made it easy for you to walk away."

"How the fuck can you say that?"

She licked her lips and spoke in a measured tone. "The kittens. You asked what I used them for, and I told you they weren't to be used. You just love them. But you also must feed them and take care of them. There is a duty you must serve to those you love. It's different because the order didn't love you. I love my family, and I have to think of others, not just myself."

My tone turned as cold as my insides. "That's bullshit. Love doesn't exist. It's a weapon people use to get what they want."

"That's not true." A flush appeared on her cheeks, and a storm entered Kat's eyes. "You are only saying that because you've never loved anyone and no one has ever lo—"

She cut herself off before she could finish, but I knew what she meant to say. I advanced on her until her back was inches from an art-covered wall, but she stopped short to keep from hurting the pieces. Still I leaned into her space and bared my teeth.

"Go ahead. Say it. No one has ever loved me."

"I didn't mean to—"

I cut her off. "You think I'm hurt because no one has ever loved me?" My heart pounded in my chest. Heat ran to my forehead and my jaw clenched. "Princess, it's the best thing to ever happen to me. It means no one can hurt me or use me. And here you are, trying to please people for no goddamn reason, going against your every instinct to choose your own path."

"Love doesn't destroy us, Gatsby," she said in a low voice, her eyes searching mine. "It saves us."

I got the message radiating from her dark eyes, loud and clear. *I could save you.*

My hands clenched and unclenched. "You really are a sheltered princess. Love hasn't saved you. It's imprisoned you. It might even kill you."

A line formed between her brows. She didn't understand what I was saying anymore, but it didn't matter.

"Don't you want love?" she asked. "Some part of you must crave connection."

"Don't get any ideas, just because we fucked."

She flinched as if I physically slapped her. And the pain it caused me made it almost impossible to breathe. But I needed to disillusion her to what our situation was. Even though it caused a piercing pain to run through my heart.

"If I had to choose between *love*," I said, the last word with dripping derisiveness, "and going back to the Order of Luxis, a place I vowed I would die before ever returning to, I'd choose the Luxis."

I took a step back then, giving Kat space. She breathed in

deep through her nose, a cold, foreboding look on her now. "Right, I see," was all she said.

"Good. Now finish up, and we'll go." I turned and walked away, as if I didn't feel cracks forming in every part of my being. I told myself I was setting her free. Teaching her that freedom was the most important thing you could have, while making sure she didn't form any attachment to me.

Because if she found out I was the one who killed her father, she might fully break.

15

KAT

After speaking to my uncle, I hadn't planned on going to party at Syn, but now there was no way I wanted to go home to be alone with Gatsby.

He communicated in no uncertain terms I was just a roll in the hay, and he had no feelings for me, and planned to keep it that way.

And that made me angry. Angry that everyone was telling me what to do. Angry I was being told not to love, not to follow my passion.

Angry enough that when we entered the club, I directly ordered two shots and downed them both without offering him anything. The rebellious girl inside me clawed her way out. Gatsby shot me a wary look as if he knew trouble was ahead.

Leaving him behind, I sashayed my way over to the group of my artist friends, who all threw their hands up and catcalled at my entrance to congratulate me for the show. I gave a little bow, before grabbing Viet's arm and pulling her onto the dance floor. I demanded more shots, and the dancing set my skin ablaze with energy as I fell into the rhythm of the music, where nothing could touch me.

I could feel Gatsby's gaze glued to me, as usual. He continued to stalk the outskirts of the place. If he was going to watch, I'd give him a show. My hips easily found the beat of the music. I pulled one of the other artists close to me for a dance. Jackson happily obliged. I circled my fingers around his neck, getting close. Jackson pressed against me, proving to be an excellent dancer. Viet shot me a strange look from over his shoulder. As if she knew I was deliberately putting on a show. So, I closed my eyes, and ground harder against Jackson. We were just friends, but Jackson went with the flow and the music.

Then he was gone.

My feet lifted off the floor as I was bodily hoisted over someone's shoulder. "Hey, let me down." My fists fell against a familiar muscular back, my hands useless as marshmallows thrown against a brick wall.

I would have hoped that people would intervene if a girl was being abducted in the middle of a dance floor. But either half of them were laughing, seeming to think this was all a fun play, and the other half seemed to be struck by fear. I could only imagine the look Gatsby cast anyone who dared think to intervene. I caught sight of Viet suppressing a knowing smile as she turned the other cheek.

Rude. If she was going to be my friend, I'd have to have a chat with her about how we handled abductions.

The thrum of the music faded as Gatsby carried me to a dark corner of the club. He set me against the wall, trapping my body with his own. "You enjoy being a brat?"

"What are you talking about?" I glared at him with haughty disdain.

Gatsby's hand reached under my dress, his fingers instantly seeking the heat between my thighs. I gasped, shocked at the feel of his fingers hooking aside my panties and pushing up into me with no preamble. But I was ready for him. My traitorous body was always ready when he was nearby.

His action stunned me into silence, but a needy moan slipped out of me as liquid raced to meet his fingers.

"You want to punish me because I don't love you? Because I will *never* love you?" His fingers pumped inside me, sending shockwaves through me.

Though I would never admit it, he instantly claimed my body and we both knew it. Again, the part of me that was sick and tired of being treated like a porcelain doll exalted in the way he took me.

"If you don't love me, why do you care?" My words came out husky. It was so damn hard to focus. Pride was the only thing that kept me from bucking against his hand to ease the ache inside me. God, I wanted him deeper, harder. I wanted to prove him wrong, make him need me, love me. The way that I loved him. Or at the least, the idea of him, for all these years.

He obliged my unvoiced need, pushing into me deeper as his lips drew even with my ear and said, "Just because I can't love you doesn't mean I'll let anyone else touch you."

"That doesn't make any sense," I said, the last word

coming out as a squeak as he curled his fingers, hitting a spot that struck me dumb. Then he removed them, staring me dead in the eye, those sharp gray eyes pinning me in place as he sucked the glistening fingers that had just been inside of me.

My first instincts were right. This was a dangerous man. He was supposed to protect me from the demons, but who would protect me from him?

Spreading his fingers into a vee, he licked between them in the most salacious, panty-melting way, without breaking eye contact. "As long as I'm here, you're mine, princess. You got that? No one else can touch you. If you let any of these idiots touch you again, I'll fucking kill them."

"You wouldn't," I breathed.

"Princess"—he leaned in until we were breathing the same breath—"what exactly do you think the Order of Luxis had me do for them?"

A wash of cold went through my heated body.

"I was their assassin," he said with a cruel smile. "Believe me when I say I won't hesitate to cut that guy's fingers off the next time I see them touch even your elbow."

My booze-soaked brain skirted around the assassin part, unable to process that bit, and went straight for his vulnerable parts. "You're jealous," I said, lips curling into a smile.

His dark grin faded. He pressed more roughly against my body. He pulled down the top of my dress. It had bra pads sewn in, so when he yanked down the top of my dress, cool air slapped against my bare nipples. They drew into tight buds.

Gatsby's warm tongue instantly found one aching peak, fueling my desire and giving me relief at the same time. His warm, rough hand squeezed and pinched at the other.

Voices neared, even as Gatsby laved his tongue against my bare breasts in a punishing, hungry fashion.

"Omg, did you see how drunk Kelly is?"

"Do you really think she's going to go home with her ex, again?"

Panic shot through me. The bathroom was around the corner, and the girls could easily take a wrong turn and find us in the back corner, Gatsby's face buried in my naked chest. I tried to push him back, but he remained unmoved.

At the same time as I feared being found, the adrenaline fueled my desire, making me more desperate for his touch. Gatsby nipped one of my peaks and I bucked and moaned. I pulled at his hair to try and force him back up my body.

"Kelly is totally going home with him. She's addicted to that toxic asshat."

Just before they rounded the corner, Gatsby stood up, covering my body with his own. His warm hand still covered my bare breast as he made intent eye contact with me. He knew exactly what he was doing. Taking control away from me to prove a point.

"Oh, it's over here," the other girl said, ignoring us and redirecting them to where the bathroom was.

"You want me to fuck you? Right here?" Gatsby asked, curling his tongue behind his teeth.

I glared up at him, feeling far too much like his plaything, and even worse, liking it. "Take me home. Right now," I said, angrily pulling up my dress.

His brow furrowed.

"I'm not playing this game, Gatsby. You say if anyone touches me, you'll kill them? Well, in this club, with the crush of people, you'll have to kill a lot of them. So you might as well take me home right now." Setting my hands on his firm chest, I pushed him away, but not before I added in my most imperious tone, "And fuck me until neither of us can stand."

We wasted zero time. I only waved at Viet from across the club to let her know I was leaving. She didn't seem surprised. Gatsby drove us back to my house. We barely made it up the stairs to my room before we were both naked. Gatsby began to kneel before me, prepared to pleasure me with his mouth, but I yanked him back up by the hair. I was more than ready.

Knowing the house was empty, I let myself groan and be as loud as I wanted when he entered me, stretching me beyond what I thought I could take. Then he pounded into me with abandon until I was full on screaming, legs up around my head. My orgasm ripped through me, blasting my insides with hot fireworks that made my back arch.

"That's my good girl. Fucking cum all over this dick," he groaned, still rocking his hips into me.

It wasn't enough. Another part of me felt empty, and it was all his fault.

"How dare you do this to me?" I rasped. Little pinpricks of feeling still lit up inside of me as my orgasm waned.

Gatsby stilled, shooting me a wary look. "Do what?"

"How dare you pull this jealousy bullshit on me after being away for so long." I rocked on his cock, the smoldering heap of coal in my belly began to spark again, but I hungered for something filthy and wrong.

He leaned down and nuzzled into my neck while gripping my hips. "No one can touch you. It drives me crazy and you knew that. You want to push me over the edge, because you know how much fucking power you have over me. How I'd fall on my knees in front of you and do any fucking thing you asked."

His words emboldened me further. I continued my

shallow rocking, my arousal wiggling and insistent for something so terribly specific. "I want to make you as crazy as you make me. How dare you turn my life upside down. How dare you make me want such filthy, naughty things."

My own wetness dripped generously, running down the crease of my backside. I grabbed his thick, beautiful cock and directed it to where I wanted it most. To where he'd left an invisible imprint with his tongue from before. I used the head of velvet steel to spread the evidence of my desire. His eyebrows quirked before a positively wicked grin spread across his face.

"Does my filthy girl want more of me in her tight little asshole?"

It was so vulgar. So unthinkable. Yet, my skin screamed in pleasure at his suggestion.

"Yes," I breathlessly confessed.

He took over, pushing my hand aside, running his hard dick up and down my sex, before pressing it into my swollen clit. I whimpered in discontent until his fingers rubbed around my second, puckered entrance.

Wonder and awe laced his words. "I thought I could scare you with how much I wanted you. If you knew I wanted to devour you, you would send me away and we'd both be safe."

"Didn't that just backfire?" I said, my voice hitching as his finger dipped inside me. I panted, my nipples hardening into painful points. But the wetness allowed his digit to slide in and out easily. A second finger joined the first. As he opened me up, he slapped his cock against my clit creating jolts of sensation and making my pussy clench.

"That's it, princess, take my fingers into that tight little hole." His hand rocked into me, evoking a completely new friction in me.

"I'm not a princess," I retorted even as fire licked me up from inside. My legs were up in the air and spread wide, his free hand holding up one of my shaking thighs.

Then his fingers disappeared and I felt the head of his mushroom head press against my virgin opening, to the place I needed him most. It was so wrong, but I needed it so bad.

"You are a princess," he said through gritted teeth as he eased into me with shallow thrusts, pushing against my tight muscles. One of my legs fell fully to the side as he gripped the other ankle, moving it to create just the right angle to sink into me. I sucked in a sharp breath as pain began to crowd out my desire. Sweat broke out all over my body as I worked to take him in, even as he moved slowly. Gatsby moved my fingers to cover my aching bud, encouraging me to find my pleasure.

Gatsby continued to talk, saying the most deliciously dirty things. "You are a princess because it's the only explanation for why I always want to fall to my knees and worship you until you've had your fill. Whether it's fucking your pretty little slit or by shoving this dick into your tight, hot asshole. Baby, I want to bend you over every surface so I can lick you from that dripping cunt to that puckered backside of yours. Only a princess could possess a pussy this good. A pussy worth killing over."

Between rubbing my own clit in that perfect spot, and his dirty words, the pain receded until I relaxed, taking in the entire head. Even with only his tip inside, I'd never felt so full, so naughty, but so good.

He sped up as he slid a little deeper into me, creating an unfamiliar pressure, and I couldn't fight it anymore.

I came screaming, sweat pouring off me, muscles shaking.

"Fuck," he roared as his hips stalled, filling me with warm liquid.

When we came to, a sweaty heap on my bed—the sheets and duvet were a tangled mess on the floor. I swiped a hand along my forehead.

He only got up to grab a towel from my bathroom, to reverently clean me up before falling back on the bed again.

Holy sweet baby goats. That had been so fucking intense.

"Are you okay?" he asked, half-sitting up, concern marring his brow.

"Yeah," I assured him, still out of breath somehow. "That was... intense."

Assured I was fine, he leaned back and covered his eyes with a hand, still recovering. "I'll fuckin' say."

The passion and feeling Gatsby inspired in me were unparalleled. If this wasn't enough to prove it, I remembered how I'd once spent two straight days working on a painting, barely remembering to eat or drink water until I'd been satisfied.

And now that painting had been the hit of the party.

He made me feel utterly possessed when he hadn't been with me, and now, it was times a hundred. I feared I would burn from the inside out, but after what I just let him do to me, it was clear I welcomed the burn.

I rolled over on my side, next to Gatsby who had closed his eyes as if succumbing to the bliss of the moment. As we lay there for a long stretch, coherent thoughts muscled their way back into my mind, cooling the haze and desire in me.

I slowly licked my lips. "You were serious about being an assassin, weren't you?"

His dark eyes snapped open to look at the ceiling.

"But if you are one of these Knights of the Light,

wouldn't all of you be considered assassins? Going out to kill demons to protect the innocent?"

I thought I saw a ghost of a smile, but it was gone before it even formed. "My brothers are heroes. They do exactly what you described. But as you've seen, my magic is flawed. It doesn't work right, and I cannot banish spirits, exorcise innocents, or create portals to travel from place to place like my brothers."

"Portals?" I breathed.

"They would be sent on missions that would last a few days, a few weeks max. I would be sent deep undercover for months at a time, having to use civilian means of travel. You saw Calan in the car with Emma. I believe he is still learning to drive, learning to read. I had to learn those skills so that I could get around and navigate my missions, since I couldn't travel by portal. But I had the more undesirable task of ridding the world of evils that some might believe to be more... gray."

I was afraid to ask the question, but it still came out. "What do you mean, gray?"

Gatsby was suddenly up and off the mattress, across the bedroom. His fingers traced one of my childhood dolls displayed on a shelf.

"There are cracks between our dimensions, between the Stygian and our world. Sometimes creatures and darkness seep through the cracks, and sometimes it's summoned. Sometimes it slips into the pores of a person and gets passed down for generations. Sometimes there is human evil that must be stopped before it can contact the dark forces, or maybe they simply got in the way of the Luxis and they needed to be removed, so I was sent to do the dirty work."

Gatsby's tone remained even as he stated the facts, but I sensed the conflict in him.

"So you killed people," I stated.

His head tilted toward me. "Does that scare you?"

"The Luxis made you do it, though, didn't they? Your order. Your bastard of a master."

He put his back to me, picking up my doll along the way, his hand unconsciously wringing her neck. "Don't do that."

"Don't do what?" I sat up, drawing my knees into my chest.

"Don't make me sound like a victim." He threw my doll to the side. It hit the wall with a loud thud. "I am not to be pitied."

"So, you wanted to kill those people?" I asked, squeezing my knees a little tighter.

He fell into silence, and again the conflict in him was palpable. Even though he was turned away, it crackled in the air, a stinging, relentless energy.

"No," he finally confessed in a low voice. "I didn't want to."

"So why didn't you run away? Stop killing people and fighting demons?" There was no accusation in my tone, only genuine neutral curiosity.

I'd been around long enough to know that where you started controlled so much of a person's life. Parents, or the lack of them, the zip code where someone is born, could determine so much of a person's life.

Gatsby looked away again, and the sharp-cut features of his perfect face struck me. His beauty was so strong it was almost painful. Like a shard of glass with sharp edges that could mercilessly slice me.

"At first, they were all I knew. There were no other options. As I was sent on more and more missions amongst civilians, it occurred to me there might be more. But by then I also knew there would be no escape. No one leaves the

Order of Luxis. No matter how far I ran, no matter how I might try to hide, they would come for me, and they would find me. Until I found a way to keep them from locating me," he said, sweeping an arm across his body. The tattoos covering his body were sigils I didn't recognize, but they appeared to be a secret language all their own. "They shield me from the magic one might use to seek something or someone."

I got up and crossed the space between us. My fingers traced the lines and curves of the tattoos, feeling the countless lines of scar tissue on his body underneath. Feeling flooded me. So much pain, so much fear, so much oppression laid into the canvas of his skin.

My words came out as a whisper. "I'm so sorry."

His hand closed around mine in a hard grip, forcing me to look up into his hard-eyed scowl.

But I didn't let that stop me. "I don't care if you're angry that I'm sorry that happened to you. I don't want you to be in pain. You didn't deserve it. You didn't deserve to be used, to be forced to do those horrible things."

Despite the look of intense concentration in his dark eyes, his grip loosened, and my hand found its way over to his heart.

"I can't—" he started and then stopped, as if deciding if he could voice the words he wanted to say. "I can't decide if you are the most foolish girl in the world, or an angel on Earth."

I would have been insulted, but the wonder in his voice let me know he believed it to be the latter. He couldn't be more wrong, but his words made me tingle. Or maybe that was his thumb caressing my hand.

"Do your brothers know?" I asked, aware I was walking onto very thin ice by asking that question.

"No," he said simply.

"Maybe you should tell them. I can tell they care about you."

The intimacy of the moment shattered. He released my hand and turned his back on me.

"And what about you? Are you going to tell your uncle you are free to do what you want? That you don't want to go to law school, and you are an artist? That you are in control of your life?"

"They don't control me. And I'm happy to support them in whatever way possible." A tiny sharp jab went through my stomach, but I pushed the feeling aside. "Family is the most important thing, and they care about you. And your brothers could be your family if you let them."

A dry laugh of disbelief escaped him. "Kat, if there is one thing I've learned, it's that no one cares about me."

Refusing to be pushed out, I pressed my bare breasts against his back, molding my naked body against his body to wrap my arms around him. "I care about you." Before he could protest, I went on. "And I saw the look in their eyes when they saw you. The sadness at seeing you on your own, the yearning for you to join them. Like they are missing a piece of their family."

"Even if what you say is true, they don't know what I've done. If they..." He paused as if weighing his words. "If they knew what I'd done, they would despise me. They would see me as the monster that needs to be banished back to the Stygian."

"You aren't a monst—"

Before I could finish, he whirled around and silenced me with his lips. His hands framed my face as he kissed me with almost painful tenderness. As if he were holding back an ocean's worth of emotion and was afraid of breaking me.

"Kat," he whispered against my lips. "I am too broken and bad for you. And you should never forget that."

He said it as if it were the most important fact in this world. But in his eyes, I could tell it broke his heart to say it. But it would break his heart still more, if I didn't believe him.

Winding my arms around him, I pressed my head against his chest. "I don't care if you are good or bad, Gatsby. I care that you stay with me."

His arms tightened around me, and we stood there for several minutes. Holding each other.

"Do you know what you are for, Gatsby?" I whispered.

"What?" he whispered back.

"To be loved."

16

KAT

The next day, it was less of a shock when I brought Gatsby down to breakfast. Though the air was no less tense. The way my family eyed the tattoos on his neck, as if they could will him out of his existence, or the very least, from the dining table.

"So Gatsby, where are you from?" my uncle asked.

"Yes, where are you from?" Dave parroted.

I had to keep from rolling my eyes. Sometimes I wondered if Dave's one wish was to be a carbon copy of my uncle.

Even Gabe set aside his tablet to hear the answer.

Gatsby didn't answer. He was shoveling food into his mouth with that single-minded efficiency again.

"He's moved around a lot," I explained for him.

"Army brat?" Gabe guessed.

Gatsby grunted. It might have been to keep from choking on his food, but my family took it to mean assent.

When Gatsby finished cleaning his plate, he sat up to find everyone looking at him. I poured myself some more French roast, as I sorted out the warring feelings I had sitting between the perfectly proper family and the man I let do bad, unspeakable things to me.

"What did you think of Kat's gallery show last night?" Gatsby asked.

Suddenly I wanted to shrink into my seat until I disappeared. The sting of my uncle's critique was still fresh.

When my uncle had seen my painting, *the Boy in Darkness*, he'd known it was the same boy I'd spoken of as a child. He sharply whispered to me that I needed to control myself before people found out. That his entire reelection was at risk. Then asked if I only cared about myself?

The shame burrowed to my core.

My uncle set his elbows on the table and threaded his fingers together. "It was... fun." His tone suggested it was anything but.

"Why weren't you two there?" Gatsby asked my cousins.

I sunk a little further in my seat, but my eyes lifted, wanting to know the answer. I'd never asked them anything like this before.

An uncomfortable silence descended on the room as Gatsby pinned them with his probing gaze.

"I had to work late." Dave glared at Gatsby before throwing me a lofty excuse. "Sorry, Katherine, had I known sooner, I would have been there.

"I sent you an email a month ago. You replied that your assistant would block off that time," I said, not believing I spoke up.

"I did?" Dave said it as if it were a question, then said more resolutely, "I did. She did. But work interfered. You know how it goes, Katherine."

I didn't. But I couldn't say his excuse surprised me.

Still, I opened my mouth again. "You couldn't be there one time? How many of your polo matches and fundraisers have I shown up to?"

"Are you really her assistant?" Gabe asked Gatsby, turning the conversation around.

"No," Gatsby said.

"He's my boyfriend," I rushed to fill in before he could say something inane, like he was my bodyguard. That led to too many questions.

The table went mute. Even Gatsby stared at me, as if he struggled to comprehend what I'd just said. I thanked the heavens he didn't contradict me.

But I knew the shock wouldn't last, so I grabbed Gatsby and yanked him up. "And we have some errands to run before tonight's soiree. And Bear needs to go for a walk, so we'll just get to it."

I ushered Gatsby out of the room. As soon as I exited the breakfast room, Bear was there, his nails clip-clopping on the wood floors, excited he heard the W word. Once I had him leashed up, we went out through the garage.

Before I could hit the button to raise the door, Gatsby grabbed my arm. I dropped the leash. Bear sat down right where he was, as if he'd given him a command to wait patiently.

"You told them I was your boyfriend," he said, searching my eyes, as if he couldn't believe his own words.

"Well yeah," I shrugged. He didn't let go of my arm, and I didn't mind. "They will be less inclined to ask questions about that than if you were my bodyguard."

Gatsby's hand dropped, and I held either arm, trying to make up for the loss of his touch.

Whatever awe had been on his face was wiped away by his usual hard scowl.

"Why don't you tell them, Kat?"

I didn't like his tone. It warned me that he was about to push into one of my soft, vulnerable parts.

"Tell them what?" I asked, taking a step back, my heel hitting the tire of my car.

His fresh, masculine scent overpowered the usual smell of rubber and concrete of the garage.

"Tell them who I am?"

Before I could respond, he went on. "Why don't you tell them the demon you saw as a girl was real? That you were right?"

My fingers dug into either arm now, as I braced myself against his demands.

"We don't need to talk about it," I said, though my voice seemed fainter than I meant it to be.

Taking hold of my arms, he pulled them away from where I had them protectively crossed. "Even before I came back, did you tell them you were right? When the gates to hell opened and demons whipped around the city streets, did you point and say, look, I was right? They do exist?"

I tried to cross my arms again, but his hands captured mine. Despite the intensity in his voice, his thumbs caressed my wrists.

"What does it matter?" I asked, trying to shrug off the ugly feelings boiling up from somewhere deep inside me, feelings I couldn't even begin to identify. But I knew if I started acknowledging them, they would swallow me whole. "My uncle rescued me from that place. I owe him everything. My family is everything to me."

Concern lined his eyes and his tone softened. "Did they say anything? Did they turn to you and say, Kat, you were right?"

I froze from my core out, turning to pure ice. I didn't try to convince my uncle of what happened that night. Even if he miraculously didn't hear it from the police, or child protective services, I'd been made a mockery of in the newspapers.

Young ingénue claims demon slayed her father before he could win the Senate.

"No." It barely passed my lips. I remembered that first night with painful clarity. Governments and military forces had to confirm the emergence of supernatural entities. An unprecedented horror had been unleashed as hellhounds and monsters made the streets run red.

I'd looked at my uncle as we watched the news together in the sitting room. His focus never wavered from the television as he sipped on his best scotch, the bottle he'd been saving for fifteen years. He drained over half the bottle that night. The world might end, after all.

I remember sitting on my hands, to keep them from trembling. Partly from anticipation, as I waited for him to acknowledge the connection. I waited for him to look at me and apologize before pulling me into his arms for a hug.

But then my anticipation turned into terror. As we continued to watch, and no one acknowledged my connection to the occurrences, I started to think I really was going mad. Maybe I had made up everything as a kid, maybe I even made up going to an institution. We never talked about it, never acknowledged it once since I came home. Maybe I was imagining what I saw on the television. Maybe my uncle and cousins were watching a news segment on the three things you shouldn't touch in a hotel room, while I fantasized there were reports on demons and hell on Earth.

I couldn't bring myself to comment or ask any questions, for fear I'd give myself away. Give away that I was sick in the head. Because even if I was screwed up in the head, I didn't want to go back to the institution.

It was a text that popped up on my phone that finally saved my sanity. Viet texted to ask if I was okay. She confessed she was terrified of what would happen next and asked if were doing anything to protect ourselves from demons.

I didn't tell her either about what happened to me as a kid, and pretended it was all new to me too.

Gatsby still held my hands, probing into me with his steely eyes.

"Why don't you tell them, Kat?"

Fear and fury rose like a tornado inside me until I shook off his hold. "Why don't you tell Calan and Leonidas about what you were forced to do for the Luxis? That you killed people for them?"

His expression cooled as he took a step back.

We stood there staring at each other for too long. Raw emotions twirling in the space between us. He pushed me. I pushed him. Were we toxic together?

Bear looked back and forth between us.

Finally, Gatsby said in an icy tone, "You like to be considered the perfect princess, don't you? You'd rather white-wash over all the cracks inside you than let anyone see. Because you need to seem better than everyone else."

I bit my lower lip. His words sliced through me. I

couldn't tell if he meant them or if he was trying to bait me. Either way, it hurt.

"I'm not better than anyone."

"Do you need to seem perfect because that's what you want? Or are you doing it because of your uncle? Does he deserve your fealty? Did you ever stop to ask yourself that?"

"Family is an automatic and normal cause for fealty," I shot back. "That is something you seem to try to reject, though. You have a shared history with your brothers, but you don't want them to see you, either. I don't know if it's because you fear their rejection, or you just can't stand an ounce of vulnerability. Either way, you are no better than me."

Woof.

Bear had waited long enough. I leaned over, grabbed his leash, and hit the door opener. It groaned open and it was as if air had been let back into the garage.

Without waiting to see if Gatsby followed, I strode out with Bear, ready to walk for as long as it took to work off the emotions he'd shaken up inside me.

Though a traitorous part of me whispered, *why didn't your uncle acknowledge you?*

17

GATSBY

I MILLED ABOUT THE GRAND BALL ROOM BEFORE THE PARTY started, staying out of the way while Kat got ready upstairs. Tonight, the function was hosted in Senator John Hart's very own home. This would be one of the biggest gatherings before the election results were tallied.

After we had walked Bear, we spent some time at the studio where Kat tried to paint, but she eventually gave up, saying she felt too self-conscious and blocked. So she decided to work out of the coffee shop below the studio for a while, as she said she needed to update her social media about what happened at the art show.

As she worked on her laptop, her expression became

grimmer with each passing minute. I peeked over her shoulder and saw she was looking at the site for Harvard Law School. Her knee jiggled as she downed a second cappuccino. At last, her Krav Maga class came. She told me under no uncertain terms she would kick my ass if I got in the way of her sparring sessions, since I threatened to cut off the fingers of the next person who touched her. She had worked her way up to full-contact sparring.

I stayed outside the dojo but kept a close eye on the trainer and her partners through the front window to make sure their touches didn't linger inappropriately. Pride swelled in me as she repeatedly dominated her opponents. Kat seemed to take out her pent-up frustration in each match. It could have been built up from the two cappuccinos, the anger and resentment I had ignited earlier, or to make up for the failed match on the street with the She.

Kat took two classes back-to-back, and then it was back to the house so she could get ready for the event. The way her skin glistened with sweat, and the ferocity in her expression made it damn near impossible to keep myself from pinning her down in the back of the car and working her in other ways until she screamed. But since our conversation in the garage this morning, she wore a big damn neon sign over her head that spelled out "Fuck off." So, I kept my distance.

In the ballroom, Kat's uncle snapped at the caterers. Dave seemed more than happy to jump down the caterer's throat after his father stepped away to chew out his campaign manager. Apparently, his speech writers did a shit job, and he was on the verge of firing everyone.

I made sure to stay out of his line of sight as I lurked about.

"They'll never let you stay," a man's voice said from behind me. I knew he was there; it just didn't matter.

"Oh yeah?" I asked, turning to face Gabe. Where Dave was all sharp angles with the flat eyes of a shark, Gabe was soft and round. Dressed in his expensive suit, it almost did the job to draw attention away from his receding hairline.

Slipping his hands in his pockets, Gabe came to stand next to me, to watch the rush of preparation. "You don't belong, you know."

I didn't answer that. Of course I didn't belong. I didn't belong anywhere.

"Do you want this life?" I asked, jerking my chin at the scene.

"Of course," he said. There was a tightness in his voice that someone else might miss. As if he were trying to convince himself. He didn't fool me, though. The way he kept his head down at the breakfast table. The way he perfectly went through the motions of agreeing and going along with his father and brother. Kat didn't seem to notice, but then he worked to detach from her as best he could. And of course, he would do his best to put as much distance between her and him. After what happened with his mother, he couldn't afford to get close to another female in his family.

"Do you remember your mother?"

Gabe stilled.

Finally, he said, "I was very young when she... left."

"Not as young as Kat." I turned to face him. "Do you miss your aunts?"

"Aunts," he said, recognizing I'd used the plural. I wasn't only referring to Kat's mother.

His hands came out of his pockets. Gabe's already white face paled, making his eyes appear even darker.

"Gabe," John snapped at his son from across the room. "Are you going to help me fix this speech, or just stand there all day?"

John's gaze lingered on me, distrust openly swimming from him. Then he turned it off as he went back to directing the event setup.

It wasn't long before people began milling in, and servers rushed around with trays of champagne.

I began to grow anxious. It was taking too long for Kat to come down. Just as I was about to go check on her, a murmur rippled through the room. When I turned around to follow its origin point, I found Kat descending the staircase.

The woman would look painfully sexy in a paper bag, and she was model perfect in the designer gowns she wore to her uncle's events all week. But now... she was a gorgeous sex vixen. The strapless black dress pushed her small but perfect breasts up like a corset. The dress flared out at the hips, falling in black waves around her. But a dangerously high slit exposed her bronzed leg. On either arm she wore black lace gloves that went up past her elbows. Gold wraps from her heels wound up her legs, like godly restraints.

There was something new and dangerous about her. Like she could eat the soul of any man or woman here. The perfect do-gooder turned into the princess of darkness, and it made my cock immediately hard.

For once, I felt like I could belong next to her. Kissing the dirt at her feet, of course, but near her nonetheless. Her veil of cultivated veneer and obedience was ripped away, revealing something far more provocative. A woman who wasn't afraid to be who she was.

Kat floated through a room of pastel colors, while men openly salivated, and women glared. A quick glance at John across the room, and I saw his face turning an unusual shade of red. Even as his lips tightened in displeasure, he tried to regain the attention of the small crowd that gathered around him.

The dark princess crossed the room to me.

The attention that had been on her, now swallowed me with greedy, probing eyes.

"What are you doing?" I murmured.

"You are my boyfriend, remember?" she said, lifting her chin with an imperious air.

"Aren't you worried about what everyone will think?" I asked.

One eyebrow arched. "Frankly, my dear, I don't give a fuck." And then an amused little smile curled on her face. I felt like I'd missed out on some inside joke. Again, my strange upbringing left me on the outside of things.

Still, I straightened and took her arm.

"How about a drink?" she suggested.

"Absofuckinglutely," I agreed, not sure if I needed it more to help distract me from the bodily reaction I had to Kat or to help distract me from the many eyes that now tracked us.

Though Kat was on my arm, she was the one who led us around. People seemed to give us a wide berth at first.

A mixture of feelings rioted through me. The discomfort of having always stayed in the shadows to suddenly be thrown in a spotlight was jarring at best. But the thrill and zing of pride that vibrated through me at having Kat on my arm was unlike any sensation I'd ever known.

Neither of us belonged here, but we belonged together.

My throat grew thick. I'd never belonged anywhere before. As Kat sipped on a glass of whiskey, neat, I dropped my hand to squeeze her waist.

No matter what horrors I faced, no matter what pathetic, dark end I met, I would never forget the night I belonged with the girl of my past and the woman of my dreams.

My heart thumped harder and harder, until I couldn't hear anything else. I swallowed hard and took Kat's drink, setting it on a nearby table.

She shot me a questioning gaze, but I simply led her to the other side of the room. Before she knew what was happening, I ushered her into the oversized washroom. The bathroom was fancier than any home I'd been in, reminding me more of a museum with its cream molding and gold-framed paintings. It smelled of lavender, but my senses were entirely honed in on the woman who permeated the space with the scent of dark honey and saffron.

Without preamble, I set her perfect ass on the sink, reaching under her dress to drag her panties off her hips and down her legs.

"Gatsby," she breathed, in shock.

I jammed the pair in my back pocket as I forcibly spread her legs with my knees. I would inhale her sweet scent later, maybe even rub one out with the black lace fabric covered in her essence.

But right now, I had the real thing. All of her perfect beauty and fierceness before me, and I couldn't wait another goddamn second.

With a quick unzip, I poised myself at her already hot, wet entrance.

"We can't," she gasped, though her expression demanded I don't dare stop. I doubt she realized how her lace-covered hands gripped my shoulders, pulling me closer.

"How can I not?" I rasped.

I pushed into her tight heat, and a half hiss, half

groan escaped me. My forehead met hers. Kat sucked in her breath and bucked against me with a helpless whimper.

Her heat burned me. Her dark eyes drilled into me, while her glistening lips held my every desire and need on them. What I would do to keep her. To be good enough for her.

A couple long strokes had us both panting. People chattered just on the other side of the door.

I would tear this world apart for Kat, rock by rock, and kill anyone who got in my way. But that's exactly how I knew I was the villain. I didn't want to save the world. I wanted to burn it at her feet, so she would know the desire she ignited in me.

The knowledge I would never be enough had me pounding into her faster, harder.

My question had been sincere. How could I not want her? How could I get her out of my dreams? How could I not want to possess her body and soul every second of my damned life?

"Gatsby," she gasped. Legs wrapped around me, drawing me closer.

I wasn't sure if this was torture or bliss to be with the one I could never have for real.

My left hand clasped the beautiful column of her neck. Dark eyes widened in surprise.

Slowly but surely clamping down on her throat so her airway became restricted, I wondered if I'd well and truly lost it.

But I knew exactly where and how hard to squeeze to break her delicate neck.

Kat's eyes rolled back into her head as she bucked harder to meet my thrusts.

I grimaced as denying myself completion turned painful.

"Don't let me destroy you, Kat," I warned. "Don't let me clip your wings. Because I'm a selfish monster." I leveled my mouth to her ear even as I squeezed her throat and pounded into her. "I just might hook my fingers in your sweet pussy and drag you down to hell with me."

Teeth sunk into my shoulder.

A woman's voice penetrated through the door, as if they were directly on the other side. "Can you believe how dry the pâté is?"

Kat screamed into my shoulder as her pussy convulsed and clenched around me. She'd latched onto my shoulder so tightly, I wondered if she was drawing blood as she whimpered and sobbed her orgasm into me. I doubled my speed, determined to draw out her pleasure.

The voice droned on, "The last party had caviar. John really must be on the downturn."

My fingers fisted at the base of Kat's skull as I ripped her head back and away from my flesh, where she was trying to hide her pleasure.

"Let them hear you," I practically snarled down at her. "I want them to know you aren't the perfect princess you've pretended to be. You're my wild, sweet slut and you come all over this dick whenever I want you to."

I reached down with my other hand, navigating around the taffeta to stroke her sensitive bud, and she screamed, still bucking against me.

The voices on the other side of the door quieted as I fucked my dark princess. But I couldn't last another moment longer. My hips stuttered as hot cum jetted into her convulsing heat.

When I finished, I half-collapsed over her. We were both

sweaty messes, and wetness slid out from where we joined.

"I—I better get back," she said in a voice as shaky as her thighs.

I slid my hand along her legs. "Fuck, Kat."

She looked up at me with glassy eyes. Her lips parted as if she were about to say something.

I craved what was on her tongue.

She'd said I wasn't meant to be used; I was meant to be loved.

My grip tightened on her legs, as I let myself fall into the fantasy. Just for this moment, I was worthy of love. I was enough. We were together at this party, and life didn't have to be a nightmare.

"Gatsby?"

"Yeah," I said, realizing my eyes were shut tight as I gripped her legs with bruising strength.

"We need to get back to the party," she said.

My bubble burst. I released her legs and pulled out. I reached over and grabbed a hand towel, cleaning her up.

"Gatsby?"

"It's nothing," I said, realizing how much my feelings were becoming transparent around her. By the way she said my name, I knew she detected the abnormality in me.

I cleaned us up and lifted Kat off the counter, setting her back on the floor. I adjusted her dress, so that it fell right again, though the back of it was a bit wrinkled now. But she smelled like sex, and the flush in her cheeks couldn't be washed away. Inside I crowed at the mark I'd left behind.

Kat shot me a seductive smile before opening the door back to the party. Her smile disappeared away in an instant.

Her uncle John stood there with a dark expression of disappointment, looking back and forth between her and me. "Having a good time, are we?"

18

KAT

MY UNCLE JOHN PINCHED THE BRIDGE OF HIS NOSE. "Fornicating in the bathroom, in easy earshot and full view of all our supporters? Have you lost your mind?"

We were in the study. The party had ended hours ago, but after he'd found me in the bathroom with Gatsby, he'd escorted me for the rest of the evening.

Gatsby had completely unhinged me until I screamed in the bathroom, and no one was left wondering where I had disappeared to.

The moment we were discovered, my uncle quietly asked Gatsby to leave the party. When I saw his shoulders bunch up as if ready for a fight, I put my hand on his chest and shook my head. He understood my silent plea and left. But I knew he'd stay nearby somehow, undetected.

My uncle tried his best to salvage my image, but I saw the looks, heard the whispers.

She's gone off the deep end.

Poor John. Some of his supporters are so offended, they are cooling off.

Who does she think she is? Sweeping in, in that dramatic number and acting like that?

Who wants to be associated with someone like that?

Did you hear, she thinks she's an artist? We all know that's code for slut.

My uncle stood from behind the desk, leaning onto his hands as if he could barely support his own weight right now. He hauled me in here as soon as he'd said his last goodbye. I suddenly felt ridiculous in my dress and longed for yoga pants and a tee.

"What do you have to say for yourself, young lady?"

Shame rolled over me in hot, intense waves. I instantly covered my stomach with my arms, but I already felt bruised and beaten by the disapproval directed at me tonight.

I opened my mouth, but an invisible hand encircled my throat and squeezed. Not like how Gatsby had, in a way that made my toes curl and orgasm come like a freight train. Shame doubled down on me following that thought, and my mouth clicked shut.

"Do you know what you cost us tonight? You do not live in a vacuum, Kat. I'm out here, working to be reelected so I can help people. Don't you care about the common good? It's already been a close campaign, and I fear tonight's escapade will shorten the gap, if we haven't fallen behind already." His fist pounded against the desk, causing me to jump. "Do you even know how you've threatened both our futures?" Then he shut his eyes tight before scrubbing a hand down his face. "No, of course you don't know. You couldn't possibly know."

When my uncle could finally meet my eye, his were bloodshot. Dark bags circled under them.

Fear shot through me. His health looked to have deteriorated at an alarming rate, and I had been the one to cause him that.

My uncle slowly rounded the desk until he stood before me. He braced his arms on the desk behind him, his weight sagging against it. "I know you didn't have a rebellious phase in high school. I waited for it. Prepared for it, but it never came. Is that what this is? You finally lashing out?" His voice darkened. "Because if you knew how important it was that I win this election, you wouldn't be so cavalier to fuck random lowlifes just to get attention and feel like a little grown-up miss. This win is as much for you as it is for me. You can't imagine how much these events mean for not just my future, but for yours. Your father would be so disappointed to see the path we are going down."

My vision swam as I fought back tears and the bile that crept up my throat.

He was right. What stupid rebellious phase had I entered that I'd let someone ruin my uncle's event?

All because Gatsby called me a fake princess, saying I only pretended to fit in when I didn't. I'd let his words get under my skin. They provoked me. They stoked a secret fire in me that felt so smothered and choked out in this lifestyle that I exploded in an inferno of ridiculousness and embarrassed everyone.

"I'm—I'm so sorry," I said, my words coming out just above a whisper. "I love my family, I love you more than anything else, and I never intended to hurt you. I'm so sorry," I repeated.

My uncle sighed, his shoulders sagging as if he couldn't hold onto his anger anymore. His anger gave way to something far worse. Disappointment. "I know you are. Now, now, no crying, let's keep our composure, eh Kat?"

I swiped at the errant tear that escaped and tried to swallow over the lump in my throat.

He walked to me and laid a hand on my shoulder. "I don't know who this man really is to you, but you need to end it. You need to cut him out of our lives if you care for this family. I'll talk to Jimi about being your date at the next function. He knows how to put on a good face and laugh things off. You and he can brush this off with elegance and just the right amount of levity."

He squeezed my shoulder, letting me know our conversation was over. I barely remember slinking out of the study, but as soon as I cleared his office, I ran up toward my room. I took the stairs two at a time, emotion threatening to burst like an overfilled water balloon.

As soon as I shut the door behind me, I grabbed a pillow from my bed and shoved it into my face where I screamed and cried until my throat was raw and my face was puffy and swollen.

I'd been so selfish and stupid. I couldn't even bring myself to turn my eyes upward to my mother's mural. She'd be disappointed in me too.

19

GATSBY

WHEN I SNUCK INTO KAT'S ROOM, I FOUND HER ASLEEP ON her bed, above the covers.

I shucked my jacket and lay down next to her.

Her eyes cracked open into bloodshot slits. Her face and lips were puffy.

My brows knotted. Had she been crying? That wasn't right.

"What's wrong?" I whispered. I lay so close our noses almost touched, but inches separated our bodies. I sensed she needed space, though I instantly wanted to crowd in and wipe out whatever was happening by kissing and touching her.

She licked her full lips, as if trying to find her voice. It took several more swallows before she croaked out, "I embarrassed my family. I've acted like a rebellious brat. I can't do it anymore."

"Do what anymore?" I asked.

She studied me with such a serious expression, I almost wondered if I was supposed to already know the answer. "Choose you over them."

I stiffened. She couldn't know how ironic that statement was. She couldn't know what I knew. How important it was for her to live for herself and not for her family.

Should I have pushed things so far, though? Had I been baiting the monster? Wanting to draw out a specific conclusion where I was Kat's savior?

Stupid pathetic fool, I heard in Master Wu's voice. *No one would choose you for anything. You are the leftover scraps of greatness, and she would never choose you. Not even if you were the last person on Earth.*

"You have to go," she said next, before I could form a response.

"I can't do that," I said in a low voice.

She sat up, so I followed suit. "You keep saying I'm in danger. That something is coming for my soul. But apart from the She, and the pixies which I feel was more a situation of wrong place, wrong time, there has been a shocking lack of paranormal activity, Gatsby." She ran a frustrated hand through her hair. "Is there even anything really coming for me?"

I licked my lips slowly, to buy time. "I believe so."

"You believe so, but you don't really know, do you?" she asked, getting up from the bed. "And based on a hunch, you are here turning my life upside down. I'm acting like a totally different person, because of you."

"Maybe you are acting like yourself for the first time?" I suggested.

Maybe you are allowing yourself to want me because that's what you really want.

"Gatsby." She sighed, covering her stomach in that way she did when she needed to close herself off from everything. Then she dropped her arms and raised her chin. "I'd rather the demon come for me face to face, than hurt my family anymore."

My body went cold where I sat, and I couldn't move. "You don't mean that."

"That's the thing. I do. I owe my family everything. Nothing in this world is more important to me than my family."

I was on my feet in an instant, my hand gripping her arm. "Kat, you don't need to sacrifice yourself for them."

"I'm not sacrificing myself," she said, shaking me off, and taking a step back. "I'm simply loving and supporting them the best way I know how. I know you can't understand this, but it's what I want. And you..." Her words faltered for a moment, but she regained her strength. "You need to leave, because you confuse me. You are making my life harder, and I need you to go."

The words gathered on my tongue, begging to be let loose.

But I love you.

A tightness twisted in my chest, bearing down against the confession. Against the words I'd never said, much less thought or felt before her.

My own words returned to me.

Love wasn't real, it was a manipulation, and I was about to try and manipulate her. I wouldn't do it. I wouldn't be that person.

Before I was aware of what I was doing, my feet carried me backward. Part of me expected her to reach for me, stop me. To say she changed her mind and then ask me to stay, to crawl in her bed and make love to her.

But her chin never dropped, and her stance never softened. Kat had made up her mind. She'd made her choice, and I wasn't it.

You are the leftover scraps of greatness. No one would ever choose you, my master's voice whispered.

I crossed the room, opened the door and left. I left Kat behind, along with the burning remnant of the only dream I ever had.

I ALMOST DIDN'T NOTICE it. Striding across the grounds of Kat's house toward where I'd hidden my motorcycle, I was completely entrenched in my traitorous feelings. But no matter how wrapped up I was, the hairs lifted from the back of my neck. A dark heat followed me. I was being stalked.

I felt the hate radiating from a set of eyes that could only be born from the fiery hell of the Stygian.

A beast was summoned to keep me away from Kat, to kill me if need be. The monster sent it. But Kat didn't want my help. I was ruining her life, and I realized she was right.

The beast wouldn't hurt Kat.

But I'd been using her as bait, and for my own selfish purposes. I was the true monster here, and the farther I got away from her, the better she would be.

And I could go back to what I knew best. Being on my own. Which was how I liked it.

20

KAT

The smile on my face was plastic. Everything felt forced, from my walk, to the pleasantries I exchanged, to the very breath in my body. But I stayed glued to Jimi's arm throughout the function put on at the Denver Botanic Gardens.

The long tent was covered in shining fairy lights, and impressive sculptures were lit up against the decorative hedges. The night air occasionally cut through the tent and swept out the overpowering perfumes of the attending ladies. The two small bars on either end could hardly keep up with the demand for booze, but the bartenders knew how to serve with a smile on their face as their tip jars nearly overflowed with crisp bills.

Jimi did exactly what Uncle John said he would. He flashed that million-dollar smile and oozed charm until people forgot to look at me with disdain or outright disgust.

With him by my side, it didn't seem to matter to anyone that John Hart's niece and surrogate daughter's outrageous behavior was splashed all over the news and social media. Jimi knew exactly what buttons to push to get people to focus on what was important. Politics, and him.

I'd attended a hundred of these parties, but this time I couldn't seem to get control of my breath. I kept holding it in, like I couldn't let it out once the night was finally over. But there were several more hours to go, so I continued to suffocate.

I longed to duck out of the tent, into the night and follow a path to a secluded corner of the gardens where no one could find me, but I stayed and performed my duty. I was the docile, agreeable, elegant niece who was so grateful her uncle had taken her in after being tragically orphaned. My uncle even chose my dress for the occasion. A black, one-shoulder velvet dress. One of my arms had a sleeve that went all the way to my wrist, leaving the other completely bare. It was perfect sophistication, making me look more grown up and serious with its straight, modern lines of design. To accommodate the hot weather, a slit rose on one side to give my legs breathing room.

This was so much harder than I expected. It was like I could see the prison I was stepping back inside of, after experiencing freedom for a brief time. I hadn't realized I'd even been in one until Gatsby showed back up in my life. Though I'd embarrassed myself and my family, I'd never felt so like myself as I had the last several days.

And now that I had to show up again and play my given role, it squeezed around me like a vice.

All the right things came out of my mouth, but I couldn't stop the insistent thoughts that pressed down on me.

"We appreciate your vote for my uncle."

I don't want to be here.

"Thank you for your donation."

I'm suffocating.

"Thank you so much for coming."

You don't know me at all.

"Wasn't my uncle's speech excellent?"

I've never been so alone.

"Hey." Jimi nudged my shoulder before handing me one of the champagnes he held. "You seem a little tense. This will help. I'll have some with you."

I gave a curt nod and sipped at the bubbles. In no time, I downed the whole glass, though I wished it were bourbon.

"That a girl," he said encouragingly.

Jimi was right. The drink did help relax me some. A sleepy warmth expanded through my body. When I stumbled, Jimi took my arm again. "Let's go find a more private place to take a break from this party."

All I could do was nod. I suddenly needed to sit down; my skin felt tingly and strange. Not bad, just strange.

Jimi led us onto a garden path, where we wove past shrubs, irises, and petunias until we reached the rose garden. At the center of the water lily pond stood a red and yellow glass sculpture of spikes that rose high into the air. It was a Chihuly, beautiful and vibrant, yet violent and prickly. It reminded me of someone I knew. My hand closed, as I wished Gatsby's strong, warm one held it.

My eyes zeroed in on a stone bench next to a statue of a

woman, and in moments I experienced the bliss that was sitting. I sighed, content as a cat.

We could still hear the chatter and music from the party, but I felt instant relief at not being under such intense scrutiny.

Jimi studied the woman's statue. "Greek, sixteenth century. When people knew how to celebrate a woman's form." His hands covered her stone bosoms, giving them a squeeze.

I couldn't even pretend to care what he was talking about. My body hummed with strange energy, and it drowned Jimi out.

"But you've got way better tits." Jimi shot me a sly smile and loosened his tie.

Time blipped and he was sitting next to me. Too close. His cologne closed in around me, and the heat of his body was oppressive. A hand roughly squeezed one of my breasts.

I batted his hand away.

"Jimi, stop," I said. My words come out a little slurred.

He giggled, an unnatural, off-kilter titter.

I tried to focus on what was wrong here.

"Did you... did you give me something?" I finally managed to ask, grasping a now-watery memory of him handing me a glass of champagne. Was that five minutes ago? Or had that been an hour ago?

"Yeah, to help you relax," he said. Then at seeing my expression he rushed to say, "I took some too. We must get through these dry functions somehow, right? I thought we could use some fun."

And then there he was again, his mouth attached to my neck like a sucker fish. Jimi's hands were on me, squeezing too tight, fumbling with the zipper on the side of my dress.

No, no, no, I didn't want this. I needed to push him away. I tried, but he just emitted that strange titter again before reattaching to my neck.

"Just relax, baby, I'm going to make you feel so good," he muttered. "Now that I know you are such a dirty little slut, I know exactly what you need."

My stomach churned. Gatsby had called me worse, but this was all wrong. It made me feel sick to my stomach.

"You need a big fucking dick to stick down that naughty throat, just yards from everyone else at the party. That way you won't scream and make a scene like the cunt you are."

"Jimi, stop," I said louder, hoping I wouldn't have to knee his balls into his throat. Though that option was becoming the far more appealing one. The situation was fast growing out of hand, and I felt disconnected from my body in a very bad way.

He gripped my arm and forced me to lie back on the bench with surprising strength. Or was I just woozy from whatever he'd given me? He pushed my dress up. Then a zipper opened with an audible rip. I twisted my body to try and maneuver him away, but he grabbed my hair with a sharp jerk.

"That's right, I like it when my dirty little sluts put up a fight. It always makes it more fun."

Panic choked my brain. This was actually happening. My weak hands uselessly batted against him.

Fuck. Why couldn't I wake up from this nightmare?

The feel of thick, hot flesh brushed across my bare thigh and I instantly felt sick.

A rush of cool air replaced Jimi. I pushed my dress back down as fast as I could and wrapped my arms around my stomach. In a second, I'd stop seeing double and I'd get up and run.

But when I looked up, I was struck dumb by what I saw.

It couldn't be. He wasn't real. I'd sent him away.

Even so, Gatsby stood there in all his beautiful, violent fury. Gatsby gripped Jimi by the scruff of his neck, and snarled in his face, like a pissed-off wolf.

It must have been the drugs, but I could see red energy crackle and pop all around Gatsby. My renegade angel had come back for me.

I could have cried with relief. Maybe I was, but my face was too numb to tell.

"She fucking said no," Gatsby seethed in Jimi's face.

A breath of relief went through me as I sagged off the bench and onto the ground.

Jimi shrugged out of Gatsby's grip. Then he threw a punch Gatsby easily ducked. He threw two more and Gatsby took a step back each time. Cold hatred lined his face. I recognized the look on Gatsby's. It preceded an absolute blood bath.

He continued to let Jimi throw his shots, but Jimi was unaware he was the prey, and the predator was toying with him. Right before the predator was about to tear out his jugular.

Jimi began to slow, having tired himself out. Finally, Gatsby landed a single sucker punch to his gut. Jimi doubled over and vomited. Gatsby leaned over to make sure Jimi could hear him. "You fucking touched her. You touched her like a goddamn animal, and now you are going to die, painfully."

I wanted to tell him no. Tell him not to cause more violence, but a disgusted shiver ran through me. Jimi wasn't going to stop. I wanted Gatsby to stop him.

I like it when my dirty little sluts put up a fight. It always makes it more fun.

Jimi's ugly words circled around my brain. He'd done this before. I knew it to my core.

My hands came up to squeeze either arm where I sat on the ground, and I realized I'd leaned back into the rose bushes. Their thorns ripped and scratched the flesh on my bare back and shoulders. Blood dripped down my arms.

Gatsby's fist next landed in Jimi's eye socket, and then his cheek. "You'll never touch her again. You'll never even get to look at her again because I'm going to rip out your eyes and cut off your unwelcome little prick."

All his rage had been unleashed and Jimi moved like an unnatural marionette under Gatsby's blows, they came so fast and hard.

A low threatening rumble reached my ears. At first, I thought the drugs were affecting my other senses. Had I imagined something growling? But when I looked to the side, I met with the milky white eyes of what at first appeared to be a dog. But as it crept forward from the bushes and shadows, I could see the flesh had rotted off the animal. It resembled a terrifying zombified version of a canine.

It tore across the cobblestone path, heading straight toward me. I sat frozen, unable to move.

Then my brain caught up and I scrambled to get to my feet. But my legs were Jell-O and I stumbled before falling. A frustrated scream caught in my throat. Adrenaline fought the fog of Jimi's drugs, but I was still disconnected from my body.

The animal was so close, the stench of rotting meat gagged me. The dog sailed through the air, about to pounce on me, and I knew I was dead. I was dog food. Canine kibble.

Gatsby jumped between us, directly into the dog's trajectory. When the dog collided with him, they went rolling into the rose bushes. Gatsby cried out in angry pain.

I scrambled to my unsteady feet, losing my footing twice. I had to cling to the woman statue to stay standing. The hellhound sunk its teeth into Gatsby's shoulder and wouldn't let go, even as they rolled in the thorn-filled rose bushes.

If I couldn't find a way to help him, Gatsby was going to die because of me.

21

GATSBY

THE HELLHOUND HAD BEEN STALKING ME, AND WHEN I'D gotten too close to Kat, it launched into action. Except her blood called to it. I'd just finished breaking Jimi's nose, when I saw it leap at her.

But I'd bleed myself dry before I let a drop of hers fall.

Blood gushed from the wound in my shoulder, as the piercing white hot pain of its teeth ripped my flesh to shreds.

I punched it in the face, but that only increased the hound's aggressiveness.

"Close your eyes," Kat yelled.

I instantly obeyed and felt the fallout from some kind of

spray that hissed into the night air. The hound whimpered and released me. Sharp particles of pepper caught in my throat, causing me to cough uncontrollably. I got to my hands and knees, coughing the rest of whatever that crap was out of my lungs. Angry whines came from the hellhound as it alternatively sneezed and growled.

"It's just pepper spray," Kat said with a slur. She blinked in astonishment. "Demon No-No is just pepper spray?"

"You low-rent fuck," Jimi snarled, getting up from the ground where I'd pounded him into a pulp. He bled from his nose and mouth, his left arm dangling awkwardly. I'd broken it. Hair rumpled and suit torn, I could almost see red flash in his dilated, bloodshot eyes. A glint of metal came out from his coat. Two things happened at once.

A shot rang out. My body jerked as white-hot pain seared through my already burning shoulder.

And the hellhound leapt onto Jimi. He fell back into the water lily pond below the glass statue.

It's drooling maw clamped down on Jimi's neck. Jimi kicked furiously as he thrashed and fought. With a sickening crack, blood spattered up onto the spikes of the glass statue and Jimi's legs went limp. And the only sounds were the watery, slurping sounds of the hellhound chewing on Jimi's body in the pond.

The pain in my shoulder was excruciating, so I did what I was taught. Like cutting a string, I disconnected from the pain. My mind floated above my body as I staggered to my feet.

I was shot. But it didn't matter. Nothing mattered but the mission.

And Kat was my mission. I would do the one thing, the only thing I was good for. Kill.

I raised my good hand at the hellhound that feasted on Jimi's face. Light flickered from my hand.

The hell hound didn't even raise its head as I tried to summon my powers.

You are a killing machine. This is what you do.

Still the light only flickered before I lost the small thread of power I'd grasped.

Voices neared. Someone heard the commotion or the gunshot and was coming to see what was happening.

"Fuck."

Kat was back to sitting on the ground, her eyes blinking slow and strange. Her faculties had been compromised. That fuck bag had given her something. And I had almost gotten here too late.

The hellhound had beaten me to killing Jimi. Right now, the undead canine was entirely preoccupied with using Jimi's face as a chew toy.

Knowing better than to rely on my powers to finish the job, I unsheathed the sword that hung on my back. The hellhound's nose was covered in gore and didn't notice me approach. I chopped its head off. Its skull landed in the water with a plop and a splash, smashing a water lily. The pain in my ripped-up shoulder began to pulsate, demanding to be felt. Blood covered me—mostly mine, some was Jimi's.

In a second, I was over Kat, helping her to her feet. Her legs buckled so I led her back to the bench.

More voices joined in.

My hands skimmed lightly over her skin. Warmth sparked in my palms, wherever I touched her. What I would do to take away her pain...

Deep scratches from the thorns marred her back and shoulders, but apart from that and her wooziness, she seemed to be okay.

"Princess, are you alright?" I asked, my voice husky from the fight.

She looked up at me, her brows furrowing, mouth turning into a pout. "What are you doing here? I sent you away."

My heart plummeted straight to my feet. I straightened and backed away.

"I heard it over here," a voice shouted. I could see the red and blue lights over the hedges. The police were here.

I couldn't afford to stick around. And Kat didn't want me here. Swallowing down the lump in my throat, I melted into the shadows, leaving her in the hands of the people she'd chosen.

22

KAT

I woke up in my uncle's office, wrapped in a heavy fur blanket.

"There's my girl," my uncle John said from nearby. A cold glass pressed into my hand. I stared at the brown liquid over ice.

"It's to help with the shock," he said.

"Water," I rasped, as I set the glass down on the coffee table with a shaky hand. I'd had enough alcohol to last a long time. The fuzziness was leaving my brain all too soon, but my heart pounded out of my chest as events in the garden came back to me in intense flashes.

The bite of the rose bushes. The image of my renegade angel throwing himself into danger to save me.

My uncle moved to get me a glass of water, which I greedily gulped down. Once I finished, I began to shiver uncontrollably.

Uncle John adjusted the blanket around my shoulders. "There, there. You're safe now, Katherine. The hellhound is dead."

"Gatsby?" I asked, terror striking my heart. I couldn't remember him leaving. Had the demon dog gotten him? When had I passed out?

A frown tugged at my uncle's mouth, making him look like an angry bass. He paused for a long moment as if calculating something. "He must have run off before we arrived with the police."

When I told Gatsby to leave the night before, I'd been certain he'd never be back. I thought he'd get on his motorcycle without looking back.

My drug-addled brain made it hard to comprehend he had actually showed up, and it hadn't been my imagination. I couldn't feel his touch even as he checked me for injuries; I had gone numb. But I remembered the way his face closed off when I asked what he was doing there with me. And then I blinked, and he was gone.

I stroked a hand along my shoulder and arm, expecting to feel tiny wounds and scabs from the thorns that bit into me. I found smooth, unmarred skin. Had I imagined it?

My uncle spoke again, leaning back against the side of his desk. "Do you think you can tell me what happened? I managed to convince the police you would give your statement when you felt up to it. But I need to know."

It spilled out. How Jimi spiked my drink and led me out into the garden to have some "fun." Gatsby showed up and kicked his ass right before that hell-spawned creature tried to eat me.

Now that the drugs had worn off, the horror of what almost happened reared its ugly head with new reality. I could still feel Jimi's slobbery lips, and how it felt like he was smothering me as he pushed my dress up. The unwanted flesh brushing against my inner thigh. I shuddered.

"The damn fool boy," my uncle muttered, looking off at one of the massive bookcases. "I told him this was a business event, and to keep things professional."

I blinked. "He drugged me."

My uncle shifted, as if uncomfortable. "Well, he must have tried to help relax you. But I certainly don't agree that this was the way to go about it."

"Go about it?" The shivering in my body intensified. Everything drained away from my brain, leaving a single shard of glass.

"Yes, well I'm agreeing with you that he was being inappropriate. But that's no one else's business." Hard interest glittered in his eyes. "Now would you mind telling me why Gatsby was there after you assured me you sent him away?"

That shard in my brain couldn't be ignored. "Uncle. Jimi almost raped me."

He scrunched his face up, as if I'd said something wildly inappropriate. "Katherine, let's not talk like that. It's unpleasant."

I shot to my feet, visibly shaking as the blanket fell away. "You're damn right it's unpleasant. How can you act like this?"

By his wince, I could tell I was shouting.

"Like what?"

"Like it's nothing. Like it's no big deal."

My uncle got to his feet and walked over to grab the whiskey from the desk. "Katherine, the poor boy is dead. No need to speak ill of the dead."

"Who knows if this was even the first time he's done something like this?" I said, though it came out screechy to my own ears. I knew to my core that I wasn't Jimi's first "party friend."

"Katherine," my uncle practically snapped, using his authoritative voice. "Let's not talk about this any further. It hardly matters now that Jimi is dead because of some godforsaken beast."

The shard sunk deep into my brain, and the pain was unbearable. I spun on my heels and walked out of his office. I wanted to run upstairs and change, but I was afraid. I was afraid to be in this house. Afraid to be trapped with my own thoughts. Afraid to be in my own skin. I needed to get out. I needed to leave. Run. Get somewhere safe.

But there wasn't anywhere safe for me. Because all I had was my family.

23

GATSBY

THE KNOCK AT MY DOOR TOOK ME BY COMPLETE SURPRISE. IN only my pants, I'd just finished tending to my shoulder. I didn't even have my shoes on.

No one came to see me, and if they did, they certainly didn't knock. They only crept in through the windows and cracks, and absolutely not a one of them announced their arrival.

I flung open the door, sword raised, ready to meet whatever new threat had come to drag me to hell and chew on my bones.

Instead, I was met with a shivering Kat, makeup streaked down her face from... tears? She was still in the dress I'd seen her wearing in the garden. The gown was tattered and smeared with dirt.

"Can I come in?" she asked through chattering teeth.

Her eyes slowly leveled with the sword I still held poised. Immediately setting my weapon aside, I said, "of course." I stepped back and she crossed the threshold of my hovel.

"How did you know where to find me?" I asked.

"When you took me home that first night, I was conscious enough to memorize the cross streets."

So, she found out I'd set up camp in the condemned building next door to her studio.

"Are you hurt?"

She shook her head.

No, she was upset, I could read it in her face, in the rigid way she held her body. But I didn't know what to do. I didn't know how to take care of her the way a normal man would.

Not Jimi, of course. He was a kind of evil in disguise. But a regular person would know what to do, and it pained me that I didn't.

My instinct was to touch her, hold her, but I couldn't be sure if that was just what I wanted. I couldn't afford to hurt her any further.

"What do I do?" I finally asked, cutting through the bullshit to get the information I desperately needed.

"Do you have hot water?" she asked through chattering teeth.

"Yes."

"I t-think I need a hot shower. I can't stop shivering."

My shoulders relaxed. I recognized this. She was in shock. I could handle this. I gently grasped her elbow and firmly led her toward the bathroom, kicking the front door shut along the way.

I turned on the hot water and waited with her for it to warm up. My hand still held her elbow, but we stood there staring at each other. Though I couldn't say what was happening, I felt an intense yet comforting energy fill the small space between us, as if she were always meant to be near me, and I her.

There were broken tiles along the walls, and rust spots marred the sink. Kat looked entirely out of place here. She deserved an oversized tub she could disappear into. She deserved pure white tiles and golden finishes. Basically, what my princess lived in at home. But she'd come to me.

When I'd first started squatting here, I scrubbed this bathroom until my knuckles bled. If I needed to treat any injuries, I'd need a sanitized place. I just didn't count on needing to treat the wounds inside a person.

Kat reached out, her fingers brushing just below my bandaged shoulder. Blood already spotted through the white wrappings.

The bullet Jimi shot into my shoulder had gone straight through. And I had undergone far worse injuries than a hellhound bite and a bullet would. I cleaned and wrapped my shoulder up easily enough.

"It's fine," I said, reading the question in her eyes.

Her hand fell and my chest squeezed, wanting it back already.

"Can you—I don't want to be alone," she said, glancing back and forth from the shower to me.

I released her elbow and stripped off my pants without question. She moved to do the same but slower. Risking the wrong thing, I slowly unzipped her dress and helped slide it down her body. The entire time, I never looked away from her face, letting her know I was here with her. For however long she needed me.

Steam curled around us, so I led her under the spray, following her in.

Kat sighed and closed her eyes, her shivers lessoning. Then without opening her eyes, she reached up and wound her arms around my neck, pulling me flush against her.

I swallowed against the lump in my throat. Water sluiced between us, turning her already soft skin positively silken. My mouth went dry as she molded her slick softness against my hard body.

The trust she had in me, naked, at her most vulnerable, shocked me to my core. Worst yet, it felt more right than anything else I'd ever known. I stroked down her hair and back, simply holding her to me. She laid her head against my chest. I was rock hard, my erection trapped against her soft belly, but I had no real desire to quell my sexual hunger. Something far deeper, more powerful, was happening.

I was about to ask her how she healed so quickly from the scratches on her arms and back, but I didn't get the chance. Her shoulders shook against me. It took me a second to realize she was crying. My arms tightened around her as my heart broke.

"I've got you," I murmured to her. "Everything's going to be okay." I didn't know how, and soon I'd be leaving her behind for good. But still, I knew I had to make things right before I left town. She deserved that. She deserved everything.

Kat buried her head into the crook of my neck. I held her like that for a long time. Feelings twisted and curled in my chest in ways I'd never experienced before.

When the water grew cold, I turned it off and reached for a towel, wrapping it around her body. Again, a pang of shame pierced my heart as I saw her wrapped in my paltry, thin towel. She deserved fluffy, oversized towels. But she didn't seem to mind. I led her to my mattress that lay on the floor and helped her down before wrapping my own body around hers protectively. I pulled up my white sheets, covering her further. Our legs twined, and a silent click went off in my mind as our bodies fit perfectly against each other.

We'd been intimate before, but nothing like this. The way Kat curled into me with such unquestionable trust made my chest swell to near breaking point. It made me want to be a better man. Made me want to be everything she ever needed. I was too sad, too broken, too bad to keep. But I could have this moment, and I'd have to make this last a lifetime.

"I was wrong," Kat muttered after a long time.

I didn't push, only continued to stroke her back and hold her close.

"I said I could take care of myself, but at every opportunity I've proven I can't."

"That's not true," I countered.

"Jimi drugged me and then he tried to—" She stopped speaking as a hard shiver ripped through her body.

I held her tighter.

She went on. "I don't think that was his first time doing something like that. I tried to gear up to kick him in the balls, but I couldn't do it. Because I knew him. How stupid is that? Because I wanted to be"—she choked on a sob—"polite and agreeable. To a guy who was going to force himself on me. I'm a fucking moron." She buried her head against my chest, covering her face.

"Don't say that. Don't talk about yourself like that. You want to face the reality here? He drugged you. Even I can be compromised like that. Not to mention it's one thing to strike a wooden post; it's another to sink a fist into flesh with the intent to harm."

She pulled away from my chest so I would hear her. "I go to Krav Maga all the time so that I can protect myself. But every chance I've gotten lately, I've fallen short."

I tipped her chin up with my knuckles, looking down at her with fierce conviction. "You've never fallen short of anything."

"Gatsby." She pouted at me. "This is the twenty-first century—women aren't damsels in distress anymore. This shouldn't be happening. I should be able to take care of myself. In fact, women aren't *allowed* to be damsels in distress! They revoke your feminist card. Pull it right out from your vagina and stamp you with a big bright letter T so everyone knows you are a traitor to your sex."

"I didn't understand all of that, but you do take care of yourself, in all kinds of ways. But no one can in all the ways. You are being too hard on yourself."

"You mean like how you are hard on yourself? Saying you're broken? But you're not. You don't choke, Gatsby."

The laugh that caught in my throat came out a strange wheeze.

"I don't choke," I repeated her words, though they felt like they came from far away. "I was raised to slay demons and destroy enemies for the Order of Luxis. While my brothers were sent to fight monsters and exorcise demons, I was sent to slit the throat of someone the Luxis needed dead. One year before I met you, I was sent on my first wetwork mission. I'd been trained since birth, but when I cornered my target in a public bathroom, I faltered. But the man figured out why I was there. He was four times my size, and he didn't hesitate. By the time we were done, the sinks were broken, the stalls ruined, and blood covered every-thing." I closed my eyes, still remembering the way the lights flickered as I caught sight of myself in a broken mirror, covered from head to toe in blood, baring my white teeth like an animal after winning the skirmish. The man's wide eyes stared at me with hate even in death.

"Did he get away?"

I licked my lips. "No. I killed him in the end. But at my core, I didn't want to. By hesitating, I drew out what could have been a quick, clean kill into something bloody and brutal. And I earned this." I took her hand and wrapped it around my waist to my side, over a thick, puckered scar. "He grabbed a shard of mirror from the wreckage of the bathroom and jammed it into my side, over and over. It was a miracle I didn't die. Though most of the time, I feel I did die that day and I've been a walking ghost."

Until I met you, I thought, but I couldn't bring myself to say the words.

"How old were you?" Kat asked in a quiet voice, her fingers lightly stroking the thickened tissue.

"Eleven."

She sucked in a breath. "You were so young."

"That's not the point. I'd been trained for years, but in the moment, I faltered. I couldn't do the one thing that was supposedly my entire purpose. You've been training too, but when the moment comes, we aren't always ready for it."

"You always seem ready to jump in and save the day." Before I could tear down her ridiculous fantasy, she went on. "You protected those people in the coffee shop from those creepy pixies. You saved me from the She, and now from Jimi and a hellhound."

My voice dropped as I confessed. "The hellhound wouldn't have come if I had kept my distance. It was tracking me, not you."

Kat stilled, before bringing her head up so she could look at me. "Why was it tracking you?"

"Someone sent it after me."

"The demon," she said knowingly.

It wasn't the right time to explain the monster's methods, so I sidestepped her statement. "When the demon dog saw you vulnerable and bleeding, it went for you. If I'd stayed away, you wouldn't have been in danger."

She tried to sit up, but I wouldn't let her. "If you had stayed away, Jimi would have really gotten what he wanted, and I would be in a hell of a lot worse shape."

I held her tight to me, as she shuddered. I couldn't even think about what almost happened. It made me want to pull that fucker's corpse out and smash it into bits all over again.

Soon Kat's breath evened out, and I found myself drifting off.

Just when I thought she'd fallen asleep, Kat spoke in a sleepy voice without opening her eyes. "Maybe you've been looking at your magic through the wrong lens. You said your magic is a result of a strong belief you hold. You believe you are a killer, and a demon. But I think you are a protector, a healer. Every time I'm with you, my scratches or cuts heal. Warmth spreads to the coldest, darkest parts of me. You do have magic. You just don't know how to believe in the best parts of yourself."

I drew her closer to me still. The only thing I believed was that heaven existed in her arms. And that this bliss wouldn't last. But right now, I could pretend life wasn't a nightmare and sleep with the girl who'd given me the first kindness I'd ever known, and inspired the fiercest passion in this or any dimension.

24

KAT

I woke with my nose buried in Gatsby's warm, naked chest. With a deep inhale, I surrounded myself in his comforting masculine smell that had only intensified in sleep.

Sunlight filled the room even through the tarp-covered, broken window. His face smoothed in slumber, and again I saw the little boy who had come into my home. I pushed back the hair that had fallen over his forehead and into his eyes. He let out a low contented moan but didn't wake.

Despite the horrible events of the previous night, I felt as though I'd been dipped into a large vat of warm honey and healed from the inside out. I meant what I said last night.

Though it took me time to absorb the nearly impossible fact, Gatsby healed me on more than one occasion. In more than one way. I had no doubt he was the cause for my feelings of renewal.

It made his belief that he only destroyed all the more heartbreaking.

I elongated into a full body stretch, curling my toes, pressing deeper into his hard body. His arm tightened around me, as if he were worried I would try to get away. A sly smile formed on my face as I managed to slip out of his grasp anyway. I wriggled down, until I met with his morning hardness. In this light, I marveled at the perfection of his length and even the coloring of his erection. Unable to help myself, I engulfed his mushroom tip into my mouth, suckling on his salty skin. A moan purred through me as I reveled in his taste. Gatsby's hips automatically rocked farther into my mouth, and I took him in.

A half pant, half growl alerted me that Gatsby was awake. I smiled around his delicious cock as I wrapped a hand around the base and stroked him up and down.

Strong fingers tunneled into my hair, massaging my scalp as I took my time tasting, playing, and exploring what made his hips jerk, or what drew out a long deep moan. Taking him in all the way to the back of my throat, I sped up until Gatsby was desperate to pull me away. I knew he was close, but I wouldn't stop for anything. In moments, he cried out, gripping my head forcing me to take him farther as he came. I greedily swallowed his dark, salty desire.

When I pulled away, Gatsby stared down at me in sheer wonder and reverence. I wiped the corner of my lips and shot him a sassy smile. In a moment, he hoisted me up, positioning me over him, knees on either side of his face. He devoured my lower lips like a starving man, plunging his tongue deep in me and sucking on my sensitive bud. I grabbed his hair and rode his face until I threw my head back, shuddering as spasms of pleasure wracked me.

We spent the rest of the day on the mattress, alternately making love and sleeping in each other's arms. Only once did Gatsby leave and bring back big piping-hot bags filled with enough cheese burgers and fries to feed an entire family, along with oversized bottles of water so we could rehydrate.

When the sun began to set, I knew I'd have to go home sooner or later. Who knew an abandoned, dilapidated apartment with a lone mattress could feel like a sanctuary.

"I don't want to go back," I confessed into the crook of Gatsby's shoulder. The scent of our lovemaking smelled intoxicating on his skin. "But I already asked our house-keeper to take care of Bear once today. I need to go back and do it myself now. Plus, he gets anxious when I'm gone too long."

Though I couldn't see Gatsby's face, I could sense him deliberating something.

"Maybe we could leave," he said. "Go back to grab Bear and your things and then leave town. Forget Jimi, forget your duties to your family, we can go somewhere no one knows us."

A fluttering began in my chest. Was it excitement or nervousness? I didn't know, but I didn't want to think too hard about it.

"Yes," I said, breathlessly. "Maybe just for a little while. Like a vacation."

Gatsby looked down at me, as if stunned that I'd agreed. Then he grabbed my face and kissed me hard, making me laugh. I tried to push him away so I could breathe but he wouldn't let go.

He peppered exuberant kisses down my neck as he squeezed my breasts. I slapped his hands away. "Okay, but if we're doing this, we need to go take care of Bear now. He needs to be let out and my poor baby probably hasn't gotten a milk bone all day."

It took a little longer than I planned, because he'd convinced me to have a quickie in the shower. I tried to put him off, saying he'd officially broken me, as I was deeply sore in all the right spots, and my legs were overcooked noodles. But Gatsby managed to coax my traitorous body into yet another round of desire, before giving me an orgasm around his strong hips, pressed against the cold shower tiles.

There was no way I was putting my ruined dress back on, so Gatsby gave me some clothes to borrow. I had to use a rubber band to tighten the waist of his pants around me enough so they wouldn't fall off. I climbed onto the back of Gatsby's bike and wrapped my arms around his torso. His hand covered mine a moment before he started the motor with a roar. I couldn't decide if the vibration hurt or helped with the soreness between my thighs.

When we got to my house, Gatsby drove right up to the front gate. I punched in the code, and the wrought-iron bars slid open.

I no sooner walked into the house than I was greeted by Bear. Uncle John strode into the front entrance behind Bear, with a frown on his face.

"Katherine, I've been worried sick about you."

I petted Bear's head, avoiding eye contact.

Gatsby shut the door behind us, and I sensed my uncle pause.

"Could we speak in private for a moment?" my uncle asked.

I looked over my shoulder at Gatsby, silently asking him if he would be alright. His lips thinned, but he gave a slight nod.

"Could you take Bear into the kitchen? There are milk bones in a big jar with a ceramic puppy's face on it. He deserves at least two."

Gatsby shot one parting look of suspicion at my uncle before calling Bear to follow. My big shaggy baby followed him without hesitation.

We barely stepped into my uncle's study before he launched into what he had to say. "You must allow me to apologize, Kat. The way I reacted to what happened to you... it's despicable. I've been so caught up in the election, I've forgotten what's most important of all. Family."

Then he surprised me by opening his arms up, inviting me in for a hug. For a moment, I was stunned. We weren't a family that hugged. My mother had been the one who loved to snuggle and stroke my hair, but the most I got from my uncle was the occasional pat on the back or shoulder. He was so much like my father.

The child in me had been waiting for this for so long, it overwhelmed me to be confronted with something I'd needed for years.

I rushed into his arms, and suddenly everything poured out of me in a torrent. How I'd been afraid I'd gone mad when the demons came onto our plane, and we didn't talk about what happened to me when I was a child. How the boy was real, and Gatsby was him. I told my uncle I didn't want to go to Harvard, and it was killing me inside just thinking about it.

All the heavy burdens weighing down my soul came rushing out like a never-ending waterfall. It ended with me telling him that I was going away with Gatsby for a while.

That way he wouldn't have to worry about me messing up his election.

By the end of it, I sat in one of the tufted chairs in front of his desk. He leaned against the desk, and his hands tightened their grip around mine as I told him everything.

"Oh Katherine," he said. "I'm so sorry I didn't believe you. And as for going to Harvard? Let's consider that idea tossed right out the window. And as for you and your beau, I know you want to run away, but in truth, I don't think I could stand us parting at a time like this. I need to make things up to you. Please don't leave, not yet anyway. Not like this. Let us celebrate your birthday tomorrow evening as planned, and then after that, you can embark on your next adventure. I fully support you and whatever you want."

I paused, still feeling the momentum from the plans Gatsby and I had made. Something pulled at my gut, telling me I shouldn't waste time. I should get in the car and head out in a new direction with Gatsby and Bear.

My uncle squeezed my hands again, giving me a hopeful, pleading look. "And at the party, we can announce your plans to travel and continue your path with art instead of law school. I would consider it a great favor to me, even though I know I don't deserve it. But I also want the opportunity to share who you really are, Katherine. You are right, you've always been there for me, and I'd like to prove that we can start on a new path together. Just give me one more day. I wouldn't feel right if you left like this."

I let out a deep breath. "Okay."

My uncle's face split into a smile as he hugged me.

Though the pulling in my gut only intensified, the deepest part of my heart wanted the fresh start my uncle offered. One where I could actually be myself.

"I'll go change, and then tell Gatsby we are staying one more day," I said, getting up.

"Of course." My uncle clapped his hands together, seeming genuinely pleased.

I raced up the stairs, nearly tripping over Gatsby's floppy sweatpants. In no time I'd thrown on a pair of my own shorts, one of my favorite oversized shirts that was covered in paint smears, and twisted my hair up into a clip. For the first time, I didn't get the pang of shame dressing how I wanted to. Like I was finally allowed to be myself.

Back downstairs, I searched for Gatsby in the kitchen, but only Bear was there, gnawing on a rawhide bone. I looked around more until I returned to my uncle's study and heard their voices filter into the hallway.

The door was ajar, enough for me to catch sight of Gatsby standing in front of my uncle, who sat at the desk.

"You can't get rid of me," Gatsby said in a matter-of-fact tone.

"It's all you, isn't it? You've been influencing her to act wild, using her as bait. Trying to stir things up to attract attention? Make sure the demon comes for her, so you can have a chance to fight it again?"

Gatsby was oddly silent. I waited for him to explain that I wasn't bait.

"How about I'll tell her I'm using her as bait, when you tell her about Wanda. Explain why she left?"

Who was Wanda? My uncle's wife's name had been Patricia. But they weren't talking about his runaway wife.

My uncle stood up; his hands flattened against his desk. "And when were you going to tell her that you're the one who killed her father?"

I was about to push the door open and insert myself into the situation, when Gatsby's words stopped me cold.

"She wouldn't let me close if she knew that. I'll tell her before I go."

"After you've completed your mission?" my uncle asked with a scoff. "You really don't care if the world burns, do you? You only care about ruining my campaign, and her future. She thinks you're here for her, but we both know you came for me."

"Guess you figured me out, John," Gatsby said, saying my uncle's name in a mocking tone.

I stumbled away from the door. My hand clutched at my stomach, as if it could tear out the writhing, nasty feelings.

Gatsby lied to me. He murdered my father.

And now, he wanted... my uncle?

My mind couldn't grasp what Gatsby wanted with my uncle, but it slid right into the sticky tar pit of realization that he really had killed my dad. Slit his throat. Because he was an assassin. It's what he'd been telling me, forcing down my throat; he was bad and would ruin my life.

If he hadn't killed my father, I would never have had to go to the institution. My uncle and cousins wouldn't have had to move in. I might have been able to have an entirely different life with the love of my father. I might have the sense to stay away from bad boys who could destroy me.

My vision blurred as I numbly walked back down the hallway. Betrayal seeped and sizzled into my bones. The realization I'd slept with my father's murderer a number of times made me sick. I stumbled over to a large antique vase and rounded over it, heaving the contents of my stomach. Tears burned my eyes.

I really was stupid.

Almost everyone I had ever known wanted to get close to my uncle through me. Why was Gatsby any different? Did he want money? Power?

It didn't matter.

It never mattered.

The only thing that mattered was how close I let someone get to me after a decade of guarding my innermost self. I let him shatter me, for what? For a devastatingly beautiful, fierce face, and someone who told me in no uncertain terms that he would never love me. A choked half sob, half laugh escaped me. I clapped a hand over my mouth.

I ended up in one of the half baths, washing the acid out of my mouth from the sink. My shaking hand managed to pour some mouthwash from the fancy decanter into one of the small glasses. I almost choked as I gargled it.

I was coming unhinged, and I almost yearned for the drugs they used to pump into me to keep my mind in a distant fog.

The blue liquid spattered against the white porcelain.

A cold clarity came over me. There was another way. A way to reclaim my independence and settle the score.

Without rinsing the sink out, I made my way toward the kitchen. Our chef had long gone, and it was clean, dark, and empty. I went to the knife block and pulled out the biggest one. The steel of the blade glinted. The cooks always kept the cutlery in prime sharpened condition.

I had to protect my family, my uncle, and my sanity. This time I'd make sure to kill the monster before it took anything else from me.

25

———

KAT

I waited, knowing with certainty he would come. After years of waiting, never knowing if he would return, I knew Gatsby would be here any minute.

The second his boots crossed my threshold, I slammed my bedroom door shut behind him.

Gatsby started, twisting to find me standing there, hands behind my back. I looked up at him from under my eyelashes.

His shoulders dropped a couple inches as he regarded me with hooded eyes. Lust filled them, and he reached for me. Even as my body reacted, I backed him up against the closed door. Strong hands found my hips as I brought my hand around from behind my back.

I pressed the kitchen knife against his throat. Gatsby tensed, his grip tightening on my hips as a line formed between his brows.

"You lied to me. You killed my father. You're using me as bait."

His features smoothed, not even bothering to stop me, or object.

"I'd ask if any of it between us was real, but I know what you think about people. Everyone uses each other, right? And you are no different. Did you really think it necessary to get into my pants, just to stay close to my uncle?"

Gatsby licked his lips slowly. Those sharp grey eyes regarded me with a coolness that made my blood boil. "You're right. I've been lying. I did kill your father, and if you want my full honesty, I'd do it again. Getting into bed with you wasn't the plan, but I can't say it didn't work for my purposes."

"For your purposes," I repeated.

Anticipation raced through me in an angry buzz. This was it. I faced my father's murderer, and I could kill him, right now. I could protect my family.

I could free myself of the past and continue forward, whole, new again.

"Are you scared?" I asked, wanting to hear it.

I told myself I wanted to taste his fear, relish the moment. But I was lying to myself. I knew I was stalling. My voice shook.

Instead of fear or anger, Gatsby's expression remained neutral.

"I always knew Death stayed closed by. He and I are old

friends, Kat." He spoke with such measured calm, and it drove me nuts. "He's walked by my side since I was a kid, and I've been waiting for him to come for me. And no one deserves to land the final blow more than you. It probably was always meant to be you. I destroyed your life, and you are going to give me what I've always deserved."

Gatsby pressed up against the blade. His flesh split under the knife, and blood pooled, then slid down the column of his neck. I pulled back so he wouldn't cut his own throat any deeper.

In a flash, he grabbed my wrists and whirled me around, pushing me up in the position I'd had him a moment ago.

The power had changed hands.

Still, his grip tightened on my wrist, keeping the blade to his own throat, even as his body pressed me into the door.

I swallowed hard. Tears blurred my vision.

"I did this to you," he said. "I ruined your life. Took someone you loved and made you suffer. I deserve this."

His cold expression morphed, and I could see that tortured little boy again. So filled with rage and pain, he only wanted one thing. Something I knew he'd never had. From the first moment I met him, I knew he desperately needed to be loved.

And stupid, stupid me. That ten-year-old girl had loved him in an instant.

Gatsby pushed my hand holding the knife against his throat harder, and his eyes flickered with pain as more blood dripped down. I tried to pull back, but he wouldn't let me.

"Stop," I said. It came out as a ragged plea.

His tone was biting and harsh. "Why? This is what you wanted, right? I ruined everything for you."

"Please stop," I begged, trying to tug the knife away from

his throat. Fear overpowered me as I knew if I let go, I'd watch him slit his own throat on my hand. I couldn't do it. I didn't want to see it. I didn't want to hurt him, not like this.

"Tell me what you want." His voice became a low, almost desperate rasp. "Tell me what you want, Kat, and I'll give it to you. Anything."

A hot tear dripped off my lashes and onto my cheek. "You. I want you. I love you."

The knife jerked back as he released my wrist. It clattered to the floor.

Gatsby stepped back; shock slashed across his face. "What?"

How could I still want the person who killed my own father?

Something inside me was broken and twisted. I thought if I killed Gatsby, I could be what my family wanted me to be. The perfect elegance expected from my family. But killing Gatsby wouldn't change any of that. I'd only lose the one person who ever saw me for me. Someone who saw my pain and didn't try to fix me. Because in his eyes, I'd been perfect just as myself.

Even if I could bring myself to kill the man in front of me, I couldn't kill the little boy I met twelve years ago. Those nights may have meant nothing to him, but to me, they had been everything.

"You," I repeated even as I hated myself for it. "I want you."

"Don't say that," he hissed.

I reached out toward the blood sliding down his neck. I wanted to erase the mark I'd left. He jerked back, out of reach. His eyes went wild.

Then he did the only thing he could. He ran.

He jumped right over the edge of my balcony. Shortly

after, the roar of his motorcycle trailed behind him, while I shook so hard, I fell to my knees trembling like a leaf in a storm.

I was in love with my father's killer.

I really was crazy.

26

———

GATSBY

She loves me.

Kat knows I killed her father, and she still loves me, still wants me.

The roar of my motorcycle and rushing wind filled my ears, but it couldn't drown out my thoughts, or my pounding heartbeat.

Maybe she really did need to be institutionalized. Because no one sound of mind would fall in love with me knowing so much about my past and who I am.

For fuck's sake, I killed, and destroyed lives. I should have told her how I fucked up those kids by killing their mother in front of them. Then maybe she would stop loving me.

Leaving was the best thing to do for her. But still, I couldn't leave before making one more stop.

I slowed down in front of the familiar, purple-colored house. When I went to press the doorbell, I was stopped by a sign that read, "Sleeping baby. Touch that doorbell or knock, and you die." So I went around back and slipped in through a side window off the dining room.

"Dumbass," croaked the parrot who stood atop his cage.

Choosing to ignore the damn bird, I followed the smell of cooked beef, strong seasoning, and off-key singing, and found Travis cooking dinner in the kitchen.

Not wanting to startle him, I rested a shoulder against the door jamb, crossed my arms and waited.

Travis continued to sing and hum about someone not having to be beautiful or cool to be his girl, he just wanted her extra time.

Just as he launched into kissy sounds, he turned around to see me standing there.

The high-pitched scream that came out of him was accompanied by a wood spatula flying straight at my face. I caught it midair, an inch away from my nose. The spoon end had some kind of red sauce on it. I licked it.

"Tacos?" I asked.

A thin baby wail came through the baby monitor on the counter.

Travis's expression went from bewildered to fearful.

"Are you kidding me?" Krystan shouted from upstairs. "I *just* got him to fall asleep."

Heavy footfalls came down the stairs, and the volume of a baby crying went up as they approached.

Krystan entered the room. She wore a cut-up black tee

and nearly non-existent booty shorts. Her jet-black hair was pulled up into a knot, while she rocked her crying child against her.

"I'm sorry, babe," Travis said, as she walked in with their kid. "I wasn't expecting a visitor." He shot a look in my direction as he untied his apron and pulled it over his head. It had a picture of a food smoker on it and read, "I only smoke the good stuff." Considering the guy used to be a massive pothead, I supposed it to be a joke. I set the wooden spoon down on a counter and crossed my arms again.

Krystan's dark brows furrowed at me, even as Travis took the crying babe from her arms.

"Sorry, little dude," he cooed at their baby. They'd named the baby Trystan. They explained once that it was a combo of both their names, a celebrity mashup name? I didn't get the joke. Or why they would give a child a joke name, but these two were anything but normal. And I was raised in a temple in the jungle to fight monsters, so that was saying a lot.

Trystan's wails immediately dropped several octaves, now that he was in his daddy's arms.

"What are you doing here?" Krystan asked, suspicion lacing her words. She crossed the kitchen to turn off the stove where Travis had been cooking.

"I..." This was going to be harder than I thought. I dropped my arms and stood up straight. "I need your help."

Krystan crooked her fingers at me to follow her into the dining room.

Travis sat at the head of the long, beat-up wood table that had once been Krystan's grandmother's. In fact, the whole house had belonged to Mrs. Rits until she passed away. When her gran had been alive, the entire place had been decorated with roosters. They had been on curtains, pitchers, statuettes, even the pillows. Room after room filled with cocks, until the place was nearly exploding with them. The place looked downright normal now.

The parrot flew off the cage until it was on the table. It waddled over to Trystan and began to whistle a lullaby. The baby calmed even further, reaching out to touch the parrot. The parrot nuzzled the tiny fingers with its beak.

"If only your demon buddies could see you now," I snorted.

The bird's head tilted sharply, so it could glare at me from a beady eye. "Youssss are the dumbass. The badsss one. You are the badss broken knight. Snarpsss is good now. Snarpss deserves the twinkiesss."

At that last bit, Snarp looked up at Travis at that last bit, bobbing his head hopefully.

The demon possessing the parrot was only good because it had a snack cake addiction these two idiots fed into, literally. Though since the baby came around, the demon bird seemed to have an affinity for the little one. The two were nearly inseparable.

"Gatsby, can you pull something out from that box next to you?" Travis asked. Trystan now happily slept in his father's arms.

I pulled up the heavy lid on the wooden box to find a treasure trove of Twinkies, Ho Hos, and Ding Dongs.

I fished out a Twinkie and opened the wrapper with my teeth before pulling out the yellow sponge cake.

"You are the goodsss knight, the goodestest knight," Snarp clicked and whistled.

Staring directly into his little black eyes, I shoved the entire Twinkie into my mouth. Then I flipped the demon bird... the bird.

With an angry squawk, Snarp flew at my face. I easily batted him away.

"That's enough," Krystan said in a low, yet deeply terrifying tone. She might as well have screamed it, the way her words reverberated through the room.

The bird settled back on the table but paced back and forth in agitation.

"If you guys wake the baby again, I'll shove you both so full of snack cakes you'll explode into gory confetti and cream filling."

Fuck, she could be terrifying when she wanted to be.

"Now toss me one of those snack cakes, stop pissing off my demon bird, and tell me why you are here."

I gave her a Ding Dong and reminded myself of what I had to do.

"I'm leaving town. But I need you to watch over someone for me. Someone who could be in danger."

Krystan unwrapped the chocolate cake and set it on the table. Snarp jumped on top of the cake and attacked it with vigor. His beak clacked and cut at the shell of icing as he made happy gargling sounds, gobbling down cake and frosting.

"What kind of danger?" Travis asked, leaning in.

Then it all spilled out. How I met Kat, everything that happened the night I killed her father, and how I was back because I feared the demon would return and take her soul. Things I'd never told anyone, they came out in a torrent.

I told myself it was because they needed all the information to fight what might come up. But it was more than that. The more I spoke, the more I felt the binds loosen around my soul.

I even told them about the relationship I had with Kat. I didn't go into detail, but I explained how we'd grown too close, and I was no good for her. That she'd found out what I'd done and could never trust me again.

"Lie," Krystan said. They had been silent this whole time, but she interjected with her accusation. "What? Did you forget we had our own little supernatural encounter and I'm now a human lie detector?"

"It's way cooler than seeing ghosts," Travis said under his breath.

She wheeled around to face him. "How can you say that? The ghost you see all the time is my grandma."

"True, I love your grandma, but maybe you should be the one spending a little more time reading those smutty romance novels out loud for her amusement." His cheeks flushed slightly.

We were getting off course. "I think you missed where I killed Kat's father, used her as bait, and lied to her. Kat can't trust me," I said.

"Lie," Krystan sighed.

Anger began to swell in me, and she must have seen it because she put both hands up. "Listen, I'm not saying it to piss you off. Maybe you are lying to yourself too, but all I know is deep down you know she trusts you and that you deserve that trust."

I supposed in a certain light that could be true, but it wasn't the whole of the issue. "Either way, I've made my decision. She needs to be watched over in case something happens."

"Why us?" Travis asked. "Why not Calan or Leonidas?" He blinked when I gave him a hard look. "I mean, I'm just curious, man. You've known them way longer and they are more qualified."

I dropped a thick wad of bills on the table. "Because I thought you were in the business of demon hunting." The black van out front said, in big bold letters, Whack A Ghoul.

"More like extermination, but yeah." Travis shrugged his shoulders.

A heavy sigh came from Snarp, who had rolled over on his back, nestled in the cream of the gutted snack cake. Fluffy filling and chocolate chunks decorated his body as if he were trying to camouflage himself as a Ding Dong. His body heaved with a tiny burp before he sighed again and slumped back, snoring almost instantly.

Krystan eyed my thick roll of money. "You chose us because you don't want to owe us anything. If you asked your brothers, you would feel beholden to them."

I didn't say anything, but she was right. I didn't want ties to anyone.

"But you see, here's the problem, Gatsby," she said, resting her slim fingers on the money. "We owe you." She slid the money back toward me.

"Don't be ridiculous. Take the money," I said, moving it back to her.

"How many times have we asked for help, and you showed up?" she asked.

"Don't you mean how many times was I actually of any use?" I sneered.

"Sure, you want to count only that, and leave out *all* the times you simply showed up to look into the face of some world-ending event or creature alongside us? It's still worth a hell of a lot more than this." Krystan slid the money to me again, shooting me a steely warning glare.

"It's not fair to you to ask this," I insisted, but I didn't push the money back on her again.

Travis and Krystan exchanged a look I didn't understand.

"Dude," Travis said in a soft voice. "It's not about fair. We are kind of... well... friends."

Cold shock snaked through my gut.

"I'd say family at this point, because we certainly don't always like one another and we have to deal with all the same weird crap, not to mention the shared history," Krystan pointed out, picking up the sleeping Trystan from Travis's arms.

"We help each other out," Travis added. "It's not about owing. And also, even without the money, why wouldn't we help protect someone important to you?"

Had everyone gone insane today? I told them what I was, like I had with Kat. And they still cared about me? "I killed people for the Luxis. I'm not like Calan. I'm an assassin."

"You *were* an assassin," Krystan shot over her shoulder just as she ascended the stairs with the baby. "Which makes a lot of sense in hindsight," she muttered.

"Did you put some kind of crazy drugs into your tacos?" I asked Travis, hearing my own voice rise as I jerked to my feet. "Why is no one getting this? I'm a bad person. I've done bad things. I'm no better than the monsters. I've destroyed families. I killed a mother in front of her kids not two months ago." I pounded my fist on the table to punctuate my point.

Thankfully, no baby wail followed my outburst. I was scared of few things, but Krystan had somehow made the list.

Travis's eyebrows shot up in surprise. "You did what now?"

Relieved I had an opportunity to convince them I was a monster, I recounted what happened. Krystan returned, to sit at the table and listen to my sins.

I told them how the kids were tied up on the bed, the carpet soaked in gasoline, and before I could remove the mom, the demon was going to turn incendiary. The woman's screaming, crying children could do nothing but watch as I slayed their mother.

Travis's face grew stony as I told him, and a bit of me found relief that he was finally believing me. Any second they would throw me out on my ass and tell me never to come back. They'd watch Kat, if for no other reason to assure her the bad man had gone.

"Jesus," Krystan breathed when I finished.

Travis rubbed his forehead.

I let out a sigh of relief. They finally got it.

"I can't believe you had to go through that, man," Travis said staring at a spot on the table, as if haunted by what I told him.

Unable to take this lunacy anymore, I pushed away from the table and ran my fingers through my hair. "You guys have this all wrong. I'm the killer here. I don't deserve your sympathy."

Krystan stood up and pointed at my seat. "You, sit down, and shut up for two minutes."

My mouth clicked shut and I did so.

"Were you the one trying to sacrifice children? No. Did you want to kill the mother? No. It was a hard decision, and you did it to save her kids."

"Calan would have—"

"Forget Calan. What if Travis or I had been in your situation? Could we have done any better? Calan has lost his powers on multiple occasions. The same thing could have happened to him. Though maybe if it had been any of us, we would have hesitated and gotten those kids hurt or worse. You hate yourself because you knew you couldn't hesitate. Gatsby, you've had a pretty shitty life. You've been abused and treated like a goddamn slave. And now you want to tell me you're the bad guy here? Since you've been on your own, have you run around and indiscriminately killed people? Summoned demons? Fuck no.

"You showed up when we called. You came when we thought the world was ending and did your best. Do you really think Travis and I are just piles of shit because we can't exorcise demons out of people? No. We do the damn job. We save people as best we can and it's not perfect. Now I'm going to go into the kitchen and make hot chocolate and cry because I'm knocked up again. And you will sit and wait until I bring it back and drink it because it is the polite thing to do. And for the last goddamn time, you are not a bad person."

Tears had gathered at the corners of her eyes, and her pale skin flushed. As soon as she finished her speech, she rushed out of the dining room and into the kitchen.

It took a moment to realize I hadn't taken a single breath during her speech. I finally filled my lungs with air and slumped back in the rickety chair. Suddenly, I felt drained.

A low chuckle brought my attention back up.

Travis shook his head with a slight smile. "I never realized it before now, but you are a lot like Krystan."

"I'm not sure if that's a compliment."

"I'm not sure if I mean it as one." Then leaning his arms on the table, he said, "She tried to do what you're doing right now—run away because she didn't think she deserved better. She ran away from my love. It fucking terrified her. But eventually she stopped running."

"Because you knocked her up."

Travis let out a long-suffering sigh. "Yes, I knocked her up. Let's totally forget the fact she got *me* drunk for that one-night stand. But come on, man, why are you really leaving? Are you afraid you are going to hurt this girl? Or maybe the truth is"—he leaned into one arm, looking me dead in the eye—"that no one can protect her better because you love her. And you are leaving because you are terrified. Terrified you don't know how to love or let love in. But how can I put this in a way you big Knights of the Light jock heads would get? It's like a muscle, or a weapon. Relationships take time and training. You don't do it perfectly every time, but you show up and fight for that other person and they show up and fight for you. Eventually you get better at it." He shot a fond look at the door to the kitchen where Krystan disappeared to.

Before I knew what was happening, I was up and across the room. "Tell Krystan I'm sorry about the hot chocolate. Please look after Kat." The front door closed soundlessly behind me.

"What do they know?" I muttered as I swung my leg over my bike. I pulled out the smushed pack of cigarettes I had stashed in my jacket pocket. I lit one up. Inhaling deeply, I let out a fog of smoke, the burn feeling good in my lungs. Then I sped off, trying to escape the stupidity of people in this city. I couldn't save them from their addled minds, but I could certainly keep from contributing to their delusions.

No matter what anyone said, I knew the truth. If I stayed, I would destroy Kat's life for a second time.

27

KAT

I spent the night at Viet's. She'd been surprised to find me on her doorstep, considering I'd always declined invitations to her place, or any of her parties. Being in her home or having her in mine felt too personal, so I'd avoided it, trying to stay on even ground.

But the ground had been ripped out from under me, and I needed a soft place to land. Despite my uncle's new understanding and support, he wasn't the person to go to about this.

"Can I come in?" I asked, rubbing my arms, feeling more uncertain than ever about what I was about to do.

Shaking off her surprise, Viet pulled me inside, instantly

wrapping me in a blanket she'd crocheted herself. The apartment smelled like her rose perfume.

While Viet made tea, I took in her glam apartment from where I sat on the cheetah-print couch. I hadn't realized Viet was a maximalist. Jewel tones exploded everywhere from her multi-colored carpet to the walls that were completely covered by ornately framed portraits and landscape paintings. Books, plants, and statuettes covered every available surface but in a way that made the space charming and inspirational. This was a place that fed the soul and wrapped me in cozy.

"I put a nip of whiskey in here," Viet said, handing me a mug shaped like a black puppy with golden eyes. She settled in next to me with her own steaming mug in hand, this one with beautiful tarot cards painted on it. Both sculpted and painted by her hand.

I wasn't sure if it was the atmosphere or the whiskey, but I came out with everything. For the first time since I was a child, I shared all my secrets with another person outside my family. Even as I spilled, I was shaking to the bone with fear at what her reaction might be. Viet only nodded her head and listened intently. A couple times, she put both our mugs on her chipped and stained coffee table to hug me.

I half-expected her to kick me out or tell me what an idiot I was.

When she didn't, I asked, "You don't think I'm crazy for loving him?"

Her big brown eyes softened. "Oh no, honey. Not at all. The kind of connection, history, and passion you describe, that's something I've only read about or seen in a painting. And I saw the way he looked at you. Like he would set the world on fire if you asked him to. Now I'm not saying the dude doesn't come with about two hundred red flags and a thousand pounds of baggage, but I can see why you've fallen for him. And to say I'm so glad he beat the unholy shit out of Jimi is putting it lightly." Her fist clenched as she gritted her teeth, as if wishing she could kick Jimi's ass too. "But if you are right, and he did kill your dad..." She paused to adjust her septum piercing. "I don't know. I feel like something's missing from the story."

"It's pretty simple, the Luxis ordered him to kill my father," I said, my heart feeling almost too heavy to beat.

"But why? What did they have against your dad? And if Gatsby doesn't work for the order anymore, why is he back and going for your uncle?"

I struggled to comprehend her questions, my head felt stuffed full of cotton, and I was dehydrated from crying.

Viet rushed on to say, "But can I say you have no idea how honored I am that you confided in me. And I promise I will honor your trust. You are safe with me, Kat. I'm so glad you felt you could come here."

At that I fully burst into tears, and she held and rocked me for a long time. We fell asleep on her couch together, watching episodes of *The Office* and eating cookies she had delivered at midnight. When I left the next morning, she promised she would come to my big birthday bash, and we would drink champagne and talk about art.

When I arrived home on my motorcycle, I was surprised to see a familiar slim, black-haired woman hanging outside the gates to my home.

I stopped and pulled off my helmet. I knew my face was a puffy mess, but I didn't care.

"Hey."

The woman patted at her bangs with a frown as if she were conflicted about something. "There's something you should know." Her tone was brash, like the last time, telling me this was how she normally spoke.

"About Gatsby?"

"No. About your family. But it's not my place, so, uh, this is for you." She handed me a wrinkled piece of paper she'd been clutching.

Wanda Schneider

4244 Foxbury Dr

Colorado Springs, CO 80902

Before I could finish reading it, she took off.

Wanda. That was the name Gatsby had used with my uncle. My uncle didn't deny knowing that name, or even seem confused or surprised by the reference.

I debated for a couple minutes before sticking my helmet back on. It was an hour and a half to Colorado Springs, so I had to leave now if I wanted to make it back to the party in time.

BY MIDMORNING, I stepped up to a house with yellow trim and sunflowers out front. The neighborhood was the definition of cookie-cutter, middle-class suburbia. My fist paused over the door.

What am I doing? I shouldn't be here.

But the feeling in my gut propelled me forward. My knuckles rapped confidently against the door.

There was a moment of silence, but then a shuffling came from inside. The door swung open, and my heart nearly beat out of my chest as I looked at a woman with a face almost as familiar as my own.

Familiar, because the woman looked exactly like my father if someone had glued a wig on his head. She had the same round nose, and deep-set eyes. There was zero doubt in my mind that they were siblings, if not twins.

"W-Wanda?" I stuttered.

"Yes?" she asked with a frown. Then she shot a pointed look at the sign next to her door that clearly stated 'No solicitors.'

"Wanda Hart?" I said, despite knowing she went by Wanda Schneider.

She frowned and took a step back, trying to shut the door. "No, you must have the wrong person."

I stopped the door with my hand. "You're... you're my aunt?" I asked, my voice shaking.

Wanda gave me a hard look, surveying me from head to toe as if trying to decide whether to slam the door in my face still.

I rushed to speak. "Please, I want to talk to you. I didn't know I had an aunt." Part of me flip-flopped in joy. "I'm Kurt's daughter."

Her face smoothed with a coldness that stemmed from pure hatred. "I'm sorry, I can't help you."

The door closed in my face.

It felt like the wind had been kicked from my chest. The shock left me stunned and rooted to the spot.

I banged on the door again with more insistence. "Wait, we need to talk. Please."

I had an aunt, but she refused to acknowledge it. Did my dad know of her? Did my Uncle John? Of course they did. How could they not know? And if they did, why was her existence completely erased? Not even the media knew about this. I'd heard Uncle John talk plenty of times about how hard it was losing his only brother, and then having his wife leave him shortly after.

Despite my persistence, Wanda didn't reappear.

A neighbor stepped out onto her front porch, shooting me a dirty look. She was on her phone and mentioned loudly about possibly needing to call the cops. I finally took a step back from the unyielding door, feeling like I'd run several miles.

The way Wanda slammed the door in my face had been so final, so dismissive.

She knew who I was and she didn't care. She wanted nothing to do with me.

My feet somehow found their way back down the pansy-edged walkway, though a numbness spread through me. The neighbor retreated back into her house, though I was sure she'd watch me from inside until she was sure I'd gone.

Before I reached the mailbox, a voice called after me. Wanda had stuck her head out of the door again. "Don't tell anyone you came here, or that you saw me," she said in a harsh tone. Then her expression softened as she added, "And if you know what's good for you, you'll get out of that house. Run far away like I did and never look back."

I opened my mouth to speak, but the door slammed again before I could get anything out.

What the hell was that about?

The hour-and-a-half drive back to Denver didn't give me any further clarity. But my guts felt like a handful of worms were wriggling in them.

Why did Gatsby know I had an aunt, and I didn't?

28

KAT

THOUGH WE'D ALREADY THROWN ONE PARTY AT OUR HOME this week, my uncle insisted we go all out again for my birthday. Except instead of the large hall, this party was set up in the gardens out back. He'd tripled the twinkle lights and brought in beautiful vintage lounge furniture and scattered it throughout the garden around the main dance floor. There were delicate, flaky napoleons, and raspberry dark chocolate mousse cakes with the special, edible golden seal from my favorite pastry chef. Exotic flower displays were everywhere, filling the evening air with sweet floral scents.

My gown was blue, the shade of the moon, and it was probably the most beautiful dress I'd ever worn. A slit rode up one side and jewels topped the pointed, sweetheart neck-line. The gathered material accentuated my hips. My hair fell in wavy curls, pulled back on one side with a crystal clip. For my twenty-third birthday I looked 1940s Hollywood glam.

Throughout the night, my uncle spoke to everyone about how he couldn't be prouder of my latest artistic success at the gallery, and we've decided that I would forgo law school to follow my passion. Maybe even travel to Europe for an extended period to study.

That last part was news to me, but I didn't hate the idea.

I needed a fresh start, and someplace far away from that damned sycamore tree. I couldn't stop checking it all day, though I knew Gatsby wouldn't be back.

It all should have felt exciting and satisfying. I didn't have to hide anymore. I could live my life and this new connection forged with my uncle appeased all my secret childhood dreams of how our family could be.

Still, I found myself escaping the fray into the house and up the stairs. I told myself I preferred to use my own bath-room, but the truth was I needed to take a breath, or twenty. I still felt suffocated amidst all those people who gave plastic smiles and nodded at the right times. Viet hadn't shown up yet, but she was never on time for anything. The party was an hour and a half in, but knowing Viet, she was probably still in her robe, curling her hair.

When I came upon the long hallway, there was already a girl sitting on a long, tufted bench. Someone else had stolen my idea of hiding from the crowd.

"Molly," I said in surprise.

My cousin's girlfriend had her hair pulled back into a French twist, and she wore a pink satin gown with puffy sleeves that made her look more like a child than a woman in her early twenties. She reminded me of Alice in Wonderland with those big blue eyes.

She jerked, as if caught doing something bad. "Oh, hi, I'm sorry, I didn't mean to—"

I waved her back down before she could get up. "No, you're fine, but can I, uh, join you for a little bit?"

Surprise remained on her face, but she scooted over, making room. I settled in next to her and let out the deep sigh I'd been holding in. We sat like that for several minutes, not speaking.

Finally, she spoke up. "Happy birthday, by the way. I'm sorry, I should have said that sooner. Are you enjoying the party?"

I shrugged and gave her a half smile. "I suppose so."

For some reason I couldn't bring myself to paint on the big smile and talk about how great things were with Molly.

"You hate these things too, don't you?" she asked.

I was taken aback by her perceptiveness. "Is it that obvious?"

She shook her head, her hands gripping the edge of the bench. "No, not at all. But I've been with your cousin for two years. It took a while to pick it up. But you are very good at playing it off. I'm miserable at it." She frowned and stared at the paisley carpet.

"But it's nice to be with Gabe, though, right?" I only said it because I was missing Gatsby by my side. What I would have given to have someone be my ally at these things. I'd feel much better when Viet got here, but it still wasn't the same.

"Don't take this the wrong way," she said before blurting out, "but he's a total kiss-ass. He hates these things too, but he'll do anything your uncle or Dave want him to do. It's like he has no mind of his own."

My eyebrows shot up. "Wow," was all I could say for a minute. I'd never heard her string so many words together, and I was surprised to find I heard a trace of an Eastern European accent.

Molly folded her hands in her lap. "Yeah, sorry. That just kind of came out. Sometimes I word-vomit the very things I'm not supposed to say." The accent was gone as if it had never been there. I realized how little I knew about my cousin's longtime girlfriend.

After a moment, I nudged her with my shoulder. "Why are you with my cousin, anyway? You could do so much better, and you wouldn't have to go to these dull parties."

She shrugged. "I guess he did all the right things, said all the right things, and he didn't take up too much of my time. But I'm beginning to see that while we kind of check the right boxes for each other, I'm wondering if I want to be the right set of checked boxes."

I let out a low whistle.

"Plus," she said, lowering her voice, "I get the sense he is hiding something from me. Like there is some dark, secret part of his life I don't know about."

The way her big blue eyes regarded me, so gravely, made an unsettled feeling swirl about in my stomach.

"I wonder if maybe he likes men?" she guessed, but she didn't seem certain about it.

"Kat?" a voice called out. It was Viet. In true form, she stood at the base of the stairs, wearing a dress with dramatic paint splatters all over it. She'd worn it in my honor, knowing she'd stand out like a sore thumb. I giggled and pulled Molly up with me.

"Sorry I'm late, girl," Viet said. "The traffic was crazy. There was an epidemic of flying demons downtown. I even passed by those demon exterminators you talked about. Whack A Ghost?"

"Whack A Ghoul," I corrected.

"Yeah, they have that big black van, like a goth Scooby Doo ride. And there were a bunch of people running by with flame throwers and shotguns. Seemed like a four-alarm fire."

"I'm glad you're okay," I said, wondering if Gatsby's brothers were on the scene, helping manage it too. Then I turned to Molly. "How about you stick with me and Viet, and we can gossip about the latest trash television or who got their Botox botched."

Molly's eyes lit up. "Oh, I just heard Jacinda got rejected by her plastic surgeon because he says she's had too much work done already."

We laughed our way back into the party and I began to enjoy myself for the first time.

WHEN IT WAS 11:45, I made my excuses and headed back inside the house to my uncle's study. He said he had a birthday gift he wanted to present to me in private.

Pushing open the door, I was surprised to see Dave and Gabe standing at his desk. They spoke in low, serious voices and they were all... holding hands? That was weird.

"Everything okay?" I asked.

They hushed and turned to me, unlinking hands.

"Of course not." My uncle smiled. "I'm afraid we were guilty of talking shop at your party. My apologies, Katherine."

The tension in the room seemed thick, though my uncle was all at ease. Dave and Gabe wore serious expressions.

"Aren't you going to wish your cousin a happy birthday?" my uncle prompted, annoyance seeping into his voice.

"Happy birthday, Katherine," my cousins mumbled, but neither of them came and hugged me. It was usually one of the two times a year I got hugs from them. On my birthday and Christmas.

Then without another word, they left out the French doors that led to the back yard.

"Are you having a good time?" my uncle asked as he went about locking the doors after them and pulling the curtains.

"Yes, thank you for the party," I said, doing my best to seem grateful.

"I really hoped it would be the best one to send you off on," he said, coming to stand by behind his desk chair.

"Send me off on? Is this present of yours about sending me to Europe?" I asked, with a nervous laugh.

The smile faded from his face. "Katherine, you care about this country, don't you?"

The sudden change of topic made me uneasy.

"Of course I do."

"And you know our family has dedicated our legacy to serving the greater good."

I shifted my weight; my palms grew sweaty for some reason. "Yes."

"Today, you are going to be a part of that legacy." Despite the inspirational words, my uncle seemed as serious as a heart attack. My own heart sped up as panic set in.

"What is this?" I asked, needing clarity right now. "What's going on?"

"Before..." he started and then switched directions. "For your birthday, I'm going to give you the truth. When you spoke of the demon in this very study, the night of your father's death, I'd known what you saw was real all along."

The room stilled and a chill spread out from my center to my fingertips. "What?"

My uncle took a seat and steepled his fingers. "You see, Katherine, in order to serve the greater good, this family has been getting help from a power greater than ourselves for quite some time. While you were dallying with that boy all those years ago, you failed to notice your father's campaign began to go poorly. His prospects for reelection were dwindling fast, so he did what all of the influencers in our ancestry have done. He called upon this entity for help."

"The demon," I managed to get out, though my mouth felt like sandpaper.

He nodded. "Indeed. In the past, we have used this means to take care of the public at large. But there is a cost. A cost we must pay if we wish to continue to do good on this Earth."

The sick feeling inside me told me I didn't want to know what the cost was.

"We must sacrifice a loved one of our family to the demon. A... family member of the female persuasion. It's an exchange so we take our rightful place so we can lead society to the right and just conclusions."

Time slowed down. My heartbeat thundered in my ears, drowning out everything else. I turned and ran to the door, jiggling the door handle, but it wouldn't give. I ran around to the French doors, passing my uncle and opened the curtains. No longer were there little square plates of glass. A wall had slid up, covering the door handle and the glass, blocking off my exit.

When the hell did that happen?

"Your cousins helped me call it forth. The entity will be

here soon," my uncle assured. "You should take a seat and relax. Have a glass of whiskey before he comes."

I began to scream for help.

"Please, Katherine," my uncle said with slight annoyance. "I wish you wouldn't. The room has been sound-proofed. An oversight that was seen to after your father's unfortunate passing."

Either he was right, or the party around the other side of the house drowned out my screams.

No one could hear me, and no one was coming.

29

———

KAT

EVENTUALLY I TIRED OF YELLING AND KICKING AT THE DOORS that wouldn't budge. I put myself across the room, as far away from my uncle as I could, panting from trying to escape. My brain buzzed with panic. This couldn't be happening.

I felt as if the wool had been pulled from my eyes. For the first time, I saw things clearly.

The way my aunt slammed the door in my face. Her parting warning to get out of the house. I should have left with Gatsby. I should have listened to my gut instead of my guilt and taken Bear and gotten the hell out of town. Gatsby was right. My perception of love was too fucked up to see how I was being twisted and used.

"The relationship I thought I had with you never existed, did it?" I asked, though I already knew the answer. "I did what I always do and painted over the ugly parts so there was only what I wanted to see. Because my parents were gone, I envisioned this loving, supportive relationship with you, but this entire time you've kept me at arm's length. The way my father did. Did he also know there might be a day that would come where he'd have to make the same choice?" Tears stung the backs of my eyes, but I refused to let them fall.

"If you had behaved," he pleaded, "If you hadn't ruined this election, everything could have been fine. I tried to make that boy go away again. I called forth a demon dog to chase him off, but yet again, everything was ruined by the both of you together. Do you know the damage that has been done to my reputation by having so many disastrous parties on the week I should be celebrating my inevitable win?"

"I'm so sorry you had to be inconvenienced by Jimi's attempt to rape me. You poor baby," I mocked.

"I should have left you in that institution," he sighed, pinching the bridge of his nose.

"What?" Another wash of cold went through me.

Dropping his arm, he gave a long-suffering look to the heavens. "I debated whether I wanted to deal with your hysterics or not. But we are family, and I took you out even though you would have been cared for there."

"No, the state had me in there. CPS had me in there until you could come get me." Even as I said it, clarity cut through me with a razor's edge. He didn't save me. He knew where I was and left me in there.

"I was eleven." It came out as a tortured whisper.

For the first time, guilt showed on his face. "I paid to make your stay comfortable until I could come for you. Katherine, you didn't know how hard it was, working abroad at the time, and I believed the round-the-clock care would help soothe you."

There it was. The thing I idolized him for, saving me from that place, was all a lie. He kept me in there like it was a daycare until it was convenient for him to pick me up. Bile rushed to my throat. I fought it back down.

"But Kat, we have to put aside our own pains and think of the greater good. As a politician, I'm a public servant. Like your father. We have to put aside the petty, insignificant needs of our own lives. And now you have the opportunity to serve the greater good too. This is your gift."

"You think sacrificing the women in your family helps you save the world? You think it makes you fit to guide or rule over anyone? I come from a line of blood-thirsty narcissists."

"Power means making hard decisions and being able to carry them through."

"Power has corrupted you into a dark, twisted monster. I'd rather spend my company with any demon over you. At least they don't deny what they are." Then the bottom dropped out from under me. "My mother?" I whispered as the realization set in.

The sadness that swept over my uncle's face was real. Which made me want to kill him with my bare hands. "Your mother was a lovely woman. And she did help bear the weight of our blessing, our curse, when we realized what Kurt would need to do to win a seat in the Senate."

I understood then that John's wife hadn't abandoned their family either. She'd secured his seat in the Senate where my father had failed. And judging by the demeanor of my cousins from ten minutes ago, they knew as well.

Their linked hands, their low monotone chanting. They were calling the demon forth together.

My vision swam. I was going to be sick.

"What about Wanda?"

His spine stiffened. "You know about Wanda?"

"Is she my father's twin?"

John nodded. "Indeed. She'd somehow found out about the cost of the greater good at a young age. She ran away from home when she was fourteen. But Kurt managed to lure her here, twelve years ago. I'm not sure how he did it, but Wanda came. It would have broken his heart if it would have had to be you at such a young age."

"Gee, isn't that nice?" I sneered.

"Don't be crass, Katherine." My uncle twisted up his face as he poured himself some of his best scotch. "I tried to throw you the best going away party I could. I'm not sure yet if we are going to explain your absence as a surprise flight to Europe where we can create a paperwork trail of you going around for months before you disappear. But then again, explaining that you were taken by a demon would put me in a better position to handle the crisis in our society today, and is more truthful in any case."

"Gatsby killed my dad to save my aunt?" I said, voicing the thing I knew to be true already.

A harsh breath forced out of his nose. "That boy has caused more problems than I can count at this point."

I'd heard enough. If I couldn't get out of the room, I'd do what I could while trapped in here. I kicked off my heels, picked up my skirts and marched over to my uncle.

He blinked just before I slammed my fist into his face.

He went careening backward off his executive's chair, rolling across the room.

For a moment I thought he'd been moaning. Then I realized he was laughing. Holding his nose and covered in his best liquor, he laughed at me. "Well now, we must go with the demon attack story. I was trying to gift you your tickets to Europe, which are already booked, when the dark spirit came. I tried to save you, but it swatted me aside." He stood again, brushing excess liquid off his jacket.

Disgust rose in me, as I realized he would use every mark I put on him as a martyr tale in the media.

My leg connected between his legs. His breath whooshed out of him as he bent over, reaching for his bruised privates. I hoped I sent his nuts straight up to his throat.

The smell of sulfur filled the room, and the lights flickered. Fear raced up my spine. A dark presence filled the room though I couldn't see it. I covered my torso and backed away until my heels hit the wall of bookshelves.

A massive book appeared from out of nowhere, hovering above my uncle's desk. Thick, black binding that dripped with tar at the edges slowly rotated in the air. The book opened almost violently and the pages flipped. I got glimpses of red script inside. Then the pages of the book stopped turning, left open on a half-filled page. I recognized my father's and uncle's names as the last several on the list. The book floated over to my uncle, who had gotten to his feet. Before I could intervene, he touched the page.

A groan of pain came out of him as blood shot forth from his finger, signing his name without him moving. The book floated away, then slammed shut with a bang that reverberated through the room and my bones.

The lights dimmed to an eerie level, and I felt a presence. My breath turned to shallow pants.

The dark mass of my nightmares seeped out from every corner of the room, gathering at the center. I shook violently as I stood before the demon I'd seen as a child all those years ago. My soul shuddered in fear for what I already knew would be a fate worse than death.

A crash came from the double doors to the study. I threw my arms to protect my face and crouched down as a blast of wood exploded into the room.

A motorcycle slid into the desk, smashing it into the solid wall behind the curtains.

Heavy boots crunched over broken detritus.

Blinking against the dust, I looked up to see Gatsby standing there in his leather jacket, without a shirt underneath. A cigarette hung from his mouth, while he gripped his sword. He looked like a renegade angel on fire, with a fury harvested from the depths of hell. But I didn't fear him. He was my savior. He always had been.

"Miss me, princess?" Gatsby asked, holding his free hand out to me.

30

———

GATSBY

Kat took my hand in an instant, and I pulled her up. The sound of ripping went through the air as she stepped on her own dress, tearing some of the skirt.

Where the fuck were Travis and Krystan? They should have been here to get Kat out and stop her uncle.

Before Kat even properly got steady on her feet, she wrapped her arms around my shoulders and kissed me soundly. When she pulled back, I didn't even bother hiding my surprise.

"If you ever tell me you're bad again, I'll spank you like a child and then command Bear to sit on you until you've come to your senses."

My gut tightened in response as feeling cascaded over me. Though I'd sped out of town, getting as far as Wyoming, Krystan and Travis's little talk had wriggled into the cracks of my brain.

The story I'd been telling myself was the one Master Wu taught me. No matter how many sigils I tattooed on to keep from being found, I kept my ghosts closer than anything.

But Travis was right. No one could protect Kat better than me because I would give up everything for her. My freedom, my life, my heart.

When I first arrived to protect Kat, it had been because I saw how close his election was. I knew John Hart would only make a deal with the family demon if he was in danger of losing. I planned to hang around and make sure Kat wasn't in danger. Then I almost actively sabotaged John's campaign, defiling his niece, doing everything I could to make her mine. To show her how much more she deserved than her shitty family. But I also believed I would be her downfall.

As long as her uncle was successful, Kat would never be in danger of being a bargaining chip. She could live in her glass house with the family she loved.

Then when I motored out of town, I believed leaving would convince John Hart there was nothing standing in the way of his election win anymore. He was ahead in the polls when I left, but the further I drove, the more I couldn't help but think he wouldn't be satisfied unless he had a sure win. I had bet his ambition against Kat's life. The second I realized how stupid a bet that was to make, I whipped my bike around and sped back. Only to find my worst fears came true.

The lights flickered as an ominous, inhuman laugh rolled through the room like thunder.

"The broken knight," a deep voice rumbled. The demon was a swirling blackness.

I pushed Kat behind me and brandished my sword at the demon. "You can't have her. So fuck off, before I'm forced to destroy you."

The laugh thundered even louder. "You cannot stop me. Her soul is mine."

Before the demon could finish its sentence, I ran and jumped on the desk, slicing through the smoke. A screech of pain went through the air, as the black mass split. My sword shimmered with red light. My magic may be faulty, but the weapon was an ancient magic artifact infused with power all its own.

"Kat, run," I commanded.

"But—"

"Do it now, princess," I yelled.

The farther she got away from the thing thirsting for her soul, the better off she was.

She turned and ran out of the room. Her uncle chased after her. I wanted to follow and pound him into a bloody pulp, but I had to first convince this demon her soul was too much trouble. Swiping my blade through the dark particles of its sulfurous evil being, the demon screeched over and over again.

Sharp blades tore down my back, and I cried out. Warm blood welled and dripped from my wounds. I wheeled around and cut through the clawed hand of the demon. Another screech as the talons evaporated.

Sweat beaded and dripped down my face and body as I continued to chop and slice at the incorporeal entity, forcing it to split over and over again. Yet the dark being continued to reform. I was only distracting it.

"You can't destroy me, knight," it hissed. "I am Azgexin."

The name hit me like a brick. The demon who tried to sacrifice those kids. It said it served Azgexin. This fucker fed on souls using proxies, dipping his dark claws in our world for too long, in too many ways.

I raised my free hand, harnessing my power to banish this thing back to hell.

Light flickered weakly from my hand.

The dark shadows gathered in front of me, red eyes opening inside it to stare at me with smug malice. Then it slammed into my chest. I flew across the room, my back cracking against the massive bookcases. I slumped to the floor, the air knocked out of me, leaving me gasping. My sword lay several feet away.

Azgexin appeared next to me, a dark tendril wrapping around my throat. I tried to grab it, but my hands fell through the dark mist even as it choked me. "You are weak and broken," it rumbled. "I will take her soul and there is nothing you can do about it. You stole a soul from me once. You won't do it again."

It took all my effort to force words out, as I continued to claw at a tentacle I couldn't grip. "She's long gone now, so if you want a soul, you'll have to take mine." I already knew it couldn't. Her uncle had signed the dark book with her soul in exchange for power. Her soul was the only thing binding the demon to this world.

But Travis and Krystan would find her; Calan and Leonidas would banish the demon. They would save her where I couldn't. As blackness began to creep into my vision, I wondered how much easier this would have been if I'd gone to my brothers for help in the first place.

"Let me go," Kat screamed.

I fought my way to consciousness to see Kat dragged back into the study by her uncle and her cousin Dave.

Canine growls mixed with Gabe's cries from the hallway. Apparently Bear disagreed with their treatment of Kat.

"Here," John yelled at the demon, shaking Kat's arm. "Take her. Take her now."

The demon released my throat only to shoot up into the air before diving straight into Kat's face, entering through her eyes, nose and mouth.

I lurched forward onto my hands and knees, hand stretched out in a futile attempt to stop it. I'd barely taken my first real breath before the demon was fully inside her.

John and Dave stepped away from her. She didn't run.

Black swallowed her brown eyes, and Kat smiled. Her lips crept up either side of her face until her unnatural grin touched either earlobe.

"No," I rasped, slamming my fists on the floor. The demon possessed her, and I had no way of getting it out of her body. Not without killing her.

31

GATSBY

Flashes of running that mother through with my sword to save her children went through my mind. There was no way for me to get the demon out of her. I couldn't exorcise shit, and it was the only way to save Kat.

Despair drowned me, as I struggled to know where to begin. How could I save her? Could I get her to Calan or Leonidas in time? I didn't know where he was. And the demon wouldn't be long before it chewed up her soul and then jettisoned out of her used body to return to the Stygian until the next deal was made.

A click penetrated through my panic and fear. Looking up from where I was on all fours, I came face to face with the barrel of John Hart's gun. "It's unfortunate you sacrificed my niece for your own dark purposes. Summoning a demon to kill her. The media will know where I couldn't save her, I could bring justice to her true murderer."

Before I could move a muscle, a shot went off, ringing through the air. I flinched.

John's eyes widened before slowly turning around. In the doorway stood Wanda Hart.

Dave lay on the floor, unconscious at her feet. She confidently gripped the handgun that was still pointed at John. He looked down at the red blossoming out from the center of his chest. He touched the blood before bringing his red, slick fingers to his face for inspection.

"Wanda?" He said her name as if he still couldn't believe she was there.

"Fuck you and fuck the men in this family," Wanda said before spitting in his direction. "I should have ended this a long time ago. Goodbye, big brother."

Then she cocked her gun and shot him again. This time he crumpled to the floor.

I moved out of the way just in time, so he didn't fall on me. On my feet, I faced the woman I'd saved all those years ago. Wanda was older and her curves fuller than when I'd seen her last.

I'd sat in that tree for weeks, waiting, watching Kurt Hart's campaign continue in a downward slump, knowing any day he would likely cave and call forth a demonic force to aid him like all his ancestors had. And I was right. The night I was supposed to meet Kat in her room to celebrate her birthday, he began the dark calling ritual. I knew then it would be the last night I'd ever see Kat.

Wanda had been terrified and furious at Kurt for tying her to a chair, about to sacrifice her soul. After I slit Kurt's throat, I cut Wanda free and helped her leave out the back French doors.

Standing over her dead brother's body, Wanda's face flickered with recognition. "You're the boy who saved me." Then she said in a firm tone, "Save my niece."

"I can't." I shook my head, knowing my worst nightmare had come true. "I can't exorcise the spirit. The only way to get it out is to kill her." The demon might as well take me too. Because there would be nothing left of me without Kat.

Bear raced into the room, barking at Kat. He knew that it wasn't his master. The demon in Kat took one look at him before raising her hand, and sent the dog flying back out in the hall. Bear cried out in fear and pain.

Anger tore through me as Wanda ran after the dog to make sure he was okay.

I had banished the demon back to the Stygian once, denying it of its prize. The fear that struck me when eleven-year-old Kat stumbled into her father's study all those years ago stabbed into my heart and bones.

The Luxis didn't care about the woman, they only cared that Kurt Hart didn't win his election. I remembered Kat's wide, watery eyes taking in what I'd done to her father, and it ignited a spark inside me.

I think you are a protector, a healer.

Kat's words returned to me. That night, I would have done anything to heal Kat's pain as she looked upon her dead father. Light sparked inside me like never before, and I was, for the first and only time, able to banish a dark spirit back to the Stygian. For her.

In the present, Kat's eyes rolled into the back of her head as the demon inside her crowed in glory, destroying her from the inside out. The entire study shook from its power.

Kat was right. I'd been trying to use my powers like a

killer. I viewed my own abilities as the power of destruction, but I'd never viewed them as creation, though I secretly longed to.

What if for once I tried to gather my magic from a place of healing rather than destruction?

Instantly my hands lit up with warmth, and I felt something spark and flow inside my core, like a golden waterfall that was never-ending. Lifting my hands, I brought them up to Kat, and focused on healing the parts of Kat that were wounded.

The shaking in the room ceased.

Kat's eyes snapped back to me, still engulfed in black. Her voice came out layered with that of the demons. "You cannot. You are the darkness like me. You will destroy her. Hurt the one person you love."

I ignored the demon's words and felt my way into Kat's energy and focused all of my being on healing her. The demon had slipped into the cracks of her soul, where the pain had gathered.

"No, what are you doing?" The demon's voice grew panicked.

Suddenly I was swept in an energy that was the most natural feeling in the world to me. And I realized how unconsciously I'd used that energy on Kat, healing her scrapes and wounds, and even pouring warmth into the cold broken bits of her soul when needed.

Kat's head jerked back and forth as her body began to seize.

Wanda raced forward and grabbed her niece from behind, holding her up, trying to steady her. Bear ran into the room as well. He paced back and forth as if wanting to help but unsure what to do. Eventually he stood up and placed his paws on Kat's chest, also helping steady her spasms.

Then I found it. The energy of the demon. It felt like a fractured wound. So, I did what felt natural, and I healed the energy.

The demon's scream was entwined with Kat's. Instead of the dark mass of energy shooting out of her body, I felt the demon's darkness disappear as I transmuted it into light. I kept going until it had all but disappeared.

Kat slumped in Wanda's arms. Her aunt laid her down on the floor. I rushed over to Kat's side. Bear licked her face, then went to lie on her legs, looking up at her face with apparent anxiety. Wanda lifted one of Kat's eyelids. Instead of blackness, her eyes were brown again.

"Is she going to be okay?" Wanda asked me, anxiety tight in her tone.

"I believe so." Kat had to wake up and reassure the both of us.

Kat groaned. "Did I fall asleep in a bubble bath again?"

A grin broke out on Wanda's face. "Guess she's feeling okay."

I barely heard her as Kat's eyes fluttered open and looked up into mine. In a second, I had her in my arms, holding onto her tightly.

And then I did something I hadn't done since I was eleven. A tear ran down my cheek, as I gripped her fiercely. "You're mine and I'm never leaving again. I don't care if I don't deserve you."

Wanda quietly got up and retreated, pulling out her phone to make a call.

Kat pulled back, brushing my tear away with her thumb. She wore a soft smile of wonder. "You are pure magic, my renegade angel."

"I love you," I said. Then I kissed her softly, as if she might break.

Kat cried as she clutched my face to hers. Her salty tears mingled with our lips. "I love you," she said into my mouth. "I always have. I couldn't stop loving you if I tried. Please don't leave me again."

"Never," I said, punctuating the promise with a kiss. Then I said it over and over again, kissing her each time as well to imprint it on her.

Bear ran around us in a frenzy, licking my face and then Kat's until we pulled Bear into the embrace. I realized I loved the mutt. Loving this big dog had been as easy as finding my true source of power. I marveled at how for the very first time in my life, things could be effortless. Once I let love in, it became the easiest thing in the world to do.

The sound of someone groaning broke our moment. Dave rubbed the back of his head, starting to sit up. Before I could get up and deal with him, a white tennis shoe stomped on his chest, forcing him back down. Wanda stood on his chest with one foot while she spoke into her phone. "Yes, I'd like to report a supernatural crime. You got a department for that yet? You do? Perfect. Send the cops. Tell them John Hart is dead and his sons need to be arrested."

32

KAT

"Why didn't you tell me?" I asked Gatsby. We snuggled on the massive sectional in my pink sweatpants and black tank top. I snuggled farther into both Gatsby's hard, warm chest and the big faux fur blanket wrapped around us. The party ended with the shocking news of my uncle's death, and they all witnessed the public arrest of my cousins.

Light flickered in the dark living room from the news channel with the coverage of the arrest. I most enjoyed the part where Gabe was arrested. When Molly heard the crimes he was being arrested for, her blues eyes widened. Gabe hung his head.

"Is it true?" she asked him over the din of people exclaiming in shock.

The steel manacles clicked around his wrists behind his back.

"Yes, it's all true. I didn't want to go along with it. They made me." Gabe didn't look her in the eye or even ask for forgiveness.

And then in a moment I found utterly shocking, Molly slapped him across the face. "You asshole," she said. "How could you do such a thing?"

Again, I could have sworn I heard a Russian accent, but her fury was far more apparent.

Viet came over and took her by the arm and they walked away together with their heads up. She'd refused to be associated with my cousin or defend him. I'd not only forged a new, deeper relationship with Viet, but I felt a new kinship with Molly.

"Why didn't I tell you?" Gatsby repeated my question. We spoke in low voices because my aunt snored softly from the other side of the sectional. She was exhausted after murdering her brother and talking to the police. She insisted she just needed to sit down a minute before driving back to Colorado Springs, but she immediately passed out. I planned to make her stay much longer. I'd use my head this time, but my heart said I may have found my true family in this ballsy woman.

Gatsby licked his lips before saying, "Because you wouldn't believe me. The way you loved your family was above and beyond what they deserved, but that didn't matter to you. You said repeatedly that you owed them everything. You're right, I was brainwashed by the Luxis, but this dickhead had also been brainwashing you. Making you think you could only live in the polished box he provided. I hoped if I helped you see you could do whatever you want, you could escape them. You are more powerful than him, more powerful than the society that has held you back. And I had no doubts that if I told you what your father did, what your uncle planned to do, you wouldn't believe me."

I chewed on my lip. Would I have believed him? I didn't know. He was right. I had this whole fantasy about what my family life was like, but it wasn't based in reality at all. If he tried to shatter the foundation of my beliefs, I'm not sure what side I would have come out on.

Gatsby spoke in an even softer voice. "And I couldn't ask you to trust me. Though it seems you trusted me more than I did."

I did know that if he'd forced me to choose between him and my family, I would have twisted in agony about what to believe.

Gatsby's thumb swept across my hand in a soothing motion. "I had only meant to watch how your uncle's election went and stay hidden but close by, like I had with your father, but I failed both times. I couldn't stay hidden. Not after you'd already seen me. You have maybe been the only person to see me. And then part of me wanted to trap you with me, so I did push you onto the wild side, knowing it would affect your uncle's election. Part of me wanted you to witness what a monster he was so you would choose me. But I was never sure I was the lesser evil."

A laugh bubbled out of me. "I'm sorry, I shouldn't laugh, but it's absurd to me you could think of yourself as evil after all you've done. You should have told me about my aunt sooner, how you saved her."

He was silent a moment. "I never viewed that night as the time I saved your aunt. I only saw it as the night I destroyed your life. I murdered your father, and you spoke about him with such love and reverence. And then I saw your devastation. In all the years since, I viewed that night as my biggest sin. I hurt the person I cared about the most."

Tears welled in my eyes and a lump formed in my throat. I had been devastated. And if Gatsby had stayed, he would have been arrested if not institutionalized too. Demons weren't common knowledge. He'd also made it clear the Luxis wouldn't have let him go. I had no idea we'd been doomed from the start.

But everything was different now. There was no more pretending to be someone I wasn't. And despite this house being rife with death and demons, without my uncle and cousins it finally felt like home for the first time. It felt like my mother's ghost walked through the halls with me, making this place a home again, like she had when I was six.

A tear dropped down my cheek. My mother's soul had been destroyed by that demon. A part of me would need time to process that horrible fact.

I intertwined my fingers with Gatsby's, needing him closer. "The only thing that matters is that you don't leave me this time."

I felt a soft kiss on my crown. "Never. I'll never leave you, Kat. I'm yours for as long as you want me."

Feeling drowsy, the intense events of the day weighing on me, I let myself drift off in the arms of the boy who I'd found hiding in my tree all those years ago. His strong arms wrapped around me, and I knew I'd finally found my lost boy.

EPILOGUE

"What do you think they're saying in there?" I asked.

Gatsby and I had gone to what he referred to as the purple house. It turned out that was where Krystan and Travis lived.

"You know, the usual male bonding," Travis assured, after pouring us all cups of steaming coffee. Krystan pulled out a can of whipped cream and went around topping off everyone's mug with a generous spurt.

Emma grunted like a caveman. "Ugh, me have feelings. Me no like."

Krystan jumped right in. "Ugga ugga, we no talk, we go kill something and ugh go eat."

Then they continued to grunt at each other in enthusiastic agreement. I laughed so hard, I doubled over.

"You girls are hi-larious," Travis said dryly, while sipping his coffee.

"What's so funny?" Calan asked, walking into the room, Gatsby close behind.

The three of us girls laughed even harder. Emma fell to

the floor and Krystan gripped the edge of the counter, while I had to cross my legs to keep from peeing myself.

"That's it," Travis said, pushing his way past us to stand by Calan and Gatsby. "I don't want to be stuck with the girls anymore. All guy time in the future"—he thumbed his own chest—"I get to be included."

Calan grunted in what sounded like begrudging agreement.

Now the three of us were positively screaming while Emma mocked his grunt.

With a parting strange glance, the men left us gasping for breath in the kitchen.

We ended up staying for lunch at Krystan's insistence, while everyone passed around Trystan, who was a snuggly baby. Though the parrot who was always on his shoulder or nearby creeped me out. Especially when I found out it was a demon. Though admittedly, its snack cake problem made it far less scary.

At the lunch table, Travis looked off to the side with a sudden intensity. "Uh-uh, okay. Oh no, sorry, I mean, yes ma'am. Of course, I will."

"Tell Gran I say hi," Krystan said without looking up from handing Trystan a cracker covered in cream cheese, which he happily smashed into his mouth.

"I need to come home with you," Travis said to me with a shrug. "Ghost gran's orders."

I shared a look with Gatsby. He seemed as confused as me, but I agreed.

Krystan stayed home with the baby while Travis followed us home in their big van.

"What did you and Calan talk about?" I asked, not expecting Gatsby to share but hoping anyway.

He didn't speak for a minute. "I told him everything. How I was never one of them. My missions were different, and about all the lives I ruined. How I hated him for being the favorite."

"And?" I asked, trying not to sound pushy, but *really* wanting to push.

"He said he had no idea. That he hates what they did to all of us, but especially to me. That he wants me to know that no matter what, he is still my brother. He would help me with anything I needed. That he hates how we were together but kept separate. And if I want to use my talents with them to fight the Stygian, I am welcome to, but even if I don't, he wants to stay in touch. Because we are... family."

"And you said..."

"I'd think about things."

I continued to stare at him. Finally, he looked over at me with a little smirk on his face. I had to fight my own smile as I settled back into my seat. He'd gotten what he needed. And where I loved Gatsby inside out, he needed his brothers. With their shared history, with their powers and abilities, I couldn't be everything to him. Just as he couldn't be every-thing to me.

I remembered then that I had drinks planned with Viet and Molly on Friday. And then Saturday, my aunt had invited us over to her house. Since coming back, she'd had a real maternal hold over me. It was like getting another mother I never knew I had.

At that, I was saddened, remembering my own mother had been sacrificed to a demon. I'd always thought her soul was up in heaven, like in the painting she'd done on the ceiling of my bedroom. But she'd gone the most horrible way I could imagine, and it made my heart clench in pain.

When we got inside the house, Travis immediately fixed his eyes on something we couldn't see.

"Is it Krystan's grandma?" I asked, knowing that was the only ghost he ever saw.

He shook his head, as he continued to watch the invisible specter and followed it up the stairs. Gatsby and I went with him.

We followed him into my bedroom, where he instantly looked up at the ceiling my mother painted and smiled.

Then he turned around to look at me, his eyes softer than before, his smile almost strangely feminine.

"Hello, my little darling," he said.

Shock went through me. "My mother used to call me that."

Travis shook his head as if trying to brush something off. "Yes, she wanted to say hello in person but that really tickles."

My heart stopped. "You are telling me my mom is here?"

Gatsby's hand squeezed mine.

"She is." Travis nodded. "She wanted me to let you know that when Gatsby destroyed the demon, she and all the other souls were set free. She's been spending a lot of time with you in the kitchen lately."

Tears gathered in my eyes. I had been feeling her presence so strongly since that night, I thought I'd only been evoking her memory to make me feel better, but no, she was really here.

Travis's head tilted in a new direction, as if interrupted. "There is another woman here. She says her name is Anne." Travis gave us an expectant look.

Gatsby and I exchanged a glance, but it was apparent neither of us knew who he was referring to.

Travis tilted his head, as if listening intently. "She says

you saved her children." Then his face smoothed of concentration as if realizing. He turned to Gatsby. "It's the woman you told us about. The one you killed to save her two kids from being sacrificed in fire."

Gatsby's hand gripped mine harder as he stiffened.

"I'm—" His mouth flapped open as if he couldn't find the words.

"She wanted you to know how grateful she is that you came and saved her babies. If it weren't for you, they all would have been killed. She needs you to stop blaming yourself in her name. She hears it every time, and needs you to forgive yourself, for the both of you."

Gatsby swallowed hard, looking like he'd eaten a hornet. I squeezed his hand back, knowing forgiving himself was one of the hardest things for him to do.

Travis excused himself after delivering the messages, saying the ghosts had gone but my mother would be around for a little while.

When Gatsby made a panicked face, Travis added on her behalf, "While keeping a respectful distance."

Lord knew I'd already begun reclaiming the big mansion as my own by beginning to redecorate the place, opening the ballroom up for art classes and, of course, screwing in most every room in the house.

My uncle may have been arrested, but the house had always been in my name and was mine to do with what I wanted.

After Travis left, we made sure to continue the tradition by taking to one of the spare bedrooms. By the end of it, we were covered in sweat, the sheets and pillows were strewn all over the room, and a bedside table was flipped over. That one was my fault.

We sat on the floor, our backs against the side of the bed.

"Fuck, Kat," Gatsby panted alongside me.

"Again?" I asked, shooting him a wicked smile.

He shot me a dark look that promised he'd resume doing all bad naughty things to me once he recovered.

He suddenly had me on my back, his hand around my throat, squeezing in that way that sent moisture toward my legs.

"You know what I'm going to use you for, princess?" he asked, a deliciously dark smile on his face.

"What?" I shot back in a sassy tone.

His hand slid around my neck to weave his fingers into my hair as he trailed soft, teasing kisses from my collarbone up to my ear.

"For love," he said in a husky voice.

I closed my eyes, as my hands clung to his back. I felt like the sun was exploding inside me at his confession.

"I love you too," I said back.

Gatsby plundered my mouth with his hot, slick tongue, as I reveled in the feel of his naked body against mine. I thought he'd been my lost boy, but he'd never leave for Neverland again. I knew Gatsby would stay here with me, and I'd love him enough to make up for all the love he'd been denied in his life.

The click-clack of nails on wood came from around the corner to stop at the threshold of the door. I smiled into Gatsby's mouth, knowing Bear would be more than willing to help too.

Want a bonus epilogue featuring Gatsby?

Visit www.hollyroberds.com and download the bonus epilogue now!

THANK YOU READER!

When I'm not writing, I'm hanging out with my reader group, Holly's Hellions, on Facebook, posting hilariously inappropriate memes, as well as sharing teasers and sneak peeks of my current WIP.

I'm also active on TikTok & Instagram.

Enjoy this steamy, action-packed urban fantasy romance!

PROPHECY GIRL

She inspired my first ever fantasy.

As I stared across the racks of wine bottles at the girl with the blonde hair cropped just at her shoulders and thick pink glasses, something stirred deep in the pit of my stomach then travelled lower. The book obscuring half her face was bound in bright colors with a man and woman embracing on the cover. Being in here every day this week has taught me that tomorrow she would come in with a different one.

Her name tag read Emma. She hadn't taken notice of me studying her, which is exactly how it was supposed to be. I was no one from nowhere.

Looking at her made me ache in places I hadn't known existed before. Like wiggling a loose tooth, I kept coming in here to feel it again. Loneliness. It had taken days for me to recognize the emotion she evoked in me. I hadn't allowed myself the self-indulgent feeling since I was ten-years-old, enduring the trials. Imagining us together both eased and worsened the loneliness, but I couldn't help myself.

The print on the blanket underneath us is covered in small blue flowers. Her eyes fasten onto mine and she can't help but lean forward, toward me, reaching for me.

The refrigerator fans were so loud, I could barely hear the country music playing in the background. The fans also kicked up the smell of wet concrete into the air, which oddly enough, I've developed a fondness for.

I reached for the wine bottle in front of me, all the while watching her liquid brown eyes race across the pages. When I walked in today, she pulled her head out of her book to smile, attempt eye contact, and welcome me into Smoky Badger Liquors. I had pulled the hood of my heavy brown coat up over my head so she couldn't have seen anything but a nod as I entered. My Masters always gave me high marks in camouflage. I'm exceptionally good at disappearing into shadow so I can watch. So I can hunt.

I was trained harder than the rest because of my bright blue eyes and dark curly hair. They explained the rare features were disadvantageous and they molded me with disciplinary force until I was able to master silent movements and veil my presence until I became a ghost in any environment. I seldom removed my hood. In North America, it was easier to blend in, but I still garnered many looks if I left the hood down, especially from women. They would hold eye contact for too long and give me mysterious smiles. It was my understanding that women are the keener observers of the sexes. I couldn't help but feel they had spotted something which made me stand out, and I couldn't have that. The hood stayed up.

I take her back to the half-built skyscraper where I spend my nights. The night air sweeps through the large rectangular cuts where floor-to-ceiling windows would eventually be installed, though no worker has appeared since I arrived in town. The white stars twinkle down at us, granting us with their divine knowing. Having Emma here with me is the utmost felicity. Her lips spread into a smile when she sees what I've brought out.

Normally, the numerous pockets on my dark khaki pants would be full of daggers, but I had to leave them behind to get through the metal detector. The first time I entered, Emma apologized for it, saying too many 'yay-hoos' had come in with their guns on their way out to or back from hunting trips. I didn't comment because I was hunting, too, although physical weapons would not be of useful aid to me this time.

I tracked my prey to this area a week ago. It had been clinging to the shadows, waiting for the perfect moment to feed again. That wasn't going to happen though. Not while I was around.

I pull out a bottle of wine, as well as a loaf of bread and a small block of cheese. In my fantasy, we sit on the blanket and eat to our heart's content. She tells me about the books she reads, though I'm sure their content is too sophisticated for my under-standing. In my fantasy, I don't eat alone.

There is a word for what I keep imagining. I'd once seen a picture of two people eating on a blanket together on a massive sign by the road when I was hunting in Ohio. They smiled and waved, their other arms locked behind each other's backs in half an embrace. I still couldn't remember the word. I eat alone and don't talk to humans because I am not worthy. Not yet anyway. But what is that word?

"Did you need help finding anything?" Emma tipped the book away from her face to ask me the question.

I realized then that I'd been holding the same bottle of wine for almost ten minutes.

Then it happened. Emma looked at me. Truly looked at me, so that no matter how expert I am at staying hidden, I was completely and utterly seen. It was both terrifying and exhilarating. My heart tripped over itself in earnest as if waving its arms and crying out, 'Yes, I see you too. I am so pleased you see me.'

I hadn't yet responded and my expression intensified toward her. The only other customer in the store glanced over from the bourbon display and raised an eyebrow in my direction. The man's dirty blonde hair framed a round face covered in scraggly facial hair not quite long enough to be a beard. His eyes were skeptical, looking at me like he knew my every thought about the woman behind the counter. His shoulders hunched, he wore his camouflage trench coat unzipped, showing off a black "Metallica" tee shirt. The coat still managed to nearly swallow up his six-foot frame. I resisted the urge to squirm.

"Um." I paused before walking toward Emma. "Yes, actually I'm not sure what I should purchase next." I shouldn't have engaged. It wasn't tactical. There was no reason to do so, but I couldn't help myself with those brown eyes boring into me.

Emma tucked a bookmark in between the pages and set it aside. As I walked over with the bottle in my hands, she straightened the over-sized shirt hanging open over a white tank top. Everything about her screamed small-town, except her eyes which were so deep I could scarcely meet them.

"What do you think of this one?" I asked, awkwardly holding out the bottle to her, almost dropping it. It's an act. I don't drop things. But it was important I come off like a yuppie. I still wasn't entirely sure what a yuppie was, but it's what a man spat at me in an alley a month ago when I grabbed him and slammed him to the ground. I claimed I'd slipped, which was a better explanation than why I really threw him to the ground, and how it would have resulted in him losing his head if I hadn't. As much as I disliked having to appear ridiculous and uncoordinated, I know how necessary it is to not appear as what I am.

Taking the bottle from me, Emma's fingers touched mine with the barest brush. Heat shot up my arm then down my back sending a shiver rolling down it with unfamiliar pleasure. Again, the fantasy assailed me in vivid color, and I desired it more than anything I'd ever wanted in my life. Someone to see me.

But it was forbidden. I was not to be seen, certainly not to know affection. I was to follow the missions wherever they took me.

Emma didn't notice my mind wander or my deliberate swallow. She examined the label, biting the inside of her cheek as she thought. "This is a Malbec, so if you want something bolder and spicier, this is your gal," she said with a smile, handing it back.

I wished she was my gal. My thoughts mimicked her term. I took back the bottle, "Oh, okay."

Her dark brows wrinkled in confusion. They were thick and dark, a striking contrast against her honey wheat hair and chestnut brown eyes. It added to the intelligence of her face. "You sure do have interesting taste in wine."

Uh oh. I put on an easy smile, "How do you mean?"

She gestured to the bottle in my hand, then tugged at the bottom of her plaid shirt. "I mean, you never drink the same kind twice. Most people come in and pick the same bottle or at least stick to the same types of wine. You've gotten everything from a cabernet to a dry white, all the way to rosés and moscatos."

Could she guess the small army of wine bottles I'd bought remained unopened, gathered at a corner of the uninhabited building I had made base camp? The fact that I'd never even had a sip of alcohol in my life was probably poking through and making me seem out of place. I'd assumed people would pick out as many different kinds of wine to collect the variety. My Masters would be disappointed in me.

I shrugged and maintained the easy smile, though my back muscles tensed.

One of the refrigerators kicked up a high whine along with a clunky rattle, making the machine sound sick. Emma looked over at it with her brow furrowed. I sniffed the air for burning rubber but detected nothing electrical. Emma stared at it a few long seconds before turning her attention back to me.

"Still figuring out what you like?" She asked.

I nodded in agreement, grateful to let her lead the conversation.

She smiled back, clearly pleased to have figured me out. "Well, there's not a lot of good stuff here. Small-town people tend to keep it sweet or in a box. Let me show you the best of the crop here and maybe that will help you decide." She came around from behind the counter. The prospect of knowing one of her favorites kicked up the speed of my heart again in hungry anticipation for something that gave me a little piece of her.

The refrigerator next to the first complaining machine rattled loudly and shook now, like it might expire any second. The other man in the store eyed the fridge from an aisle away, edging away from it.

Emma took a few steps toward the refrigerators. "That's weird. At least it's cold out, so if the fridges die, I can nestle the bottles in the snow out back." Casting a shy glance over her shoulder at me, she bit the inside of her cheek in a way that made me feel all at once restless. "I guess I shouldn't advertise where I plan to stash the unsupervised booze."

She laughed lightly, but I wasn't paying attention to her anymore.

A third refrigerator matched the clatter and screech of the first two. One of my hands fell to Emma's arm, stopping her from moving any closer. I almost didn't notice how good it felt to touch her warm, impossibly soft skin. Almost.

My gaze darted around the store. "You need to go," I instructed in a low voice.

Get Prophecy Girl now to keep reading

A LETTER FROM THE AUTHOR

Dear Reader,

Thank you for reading!

I loved revisiting the Five Orders series, and finally giving Gatsby his own story - I've known FOR SO LONG about his secret, tragic pst. There are so many of the characters in that series that are begging for their own story. So let me know if there is anyone you want to read more about!

Loved this book? Consider leaving a review as it helps other readers discover my books.

Want to make sure you never miss a release or any bonus content I have coming down the pipeline?

Make sure to join Holly's Hotspot, my newsletter, and I'll send you a FREE ebook right away!

You can also find me on my website www.hollyroberds.com and I hang out on social media.

Tiktok: https://www.tiktok.com/@hollyroberdsauthor

Instagram: http://instagram.com/authorhollyroberds

Facebook: www.facebook.com/hollyroberdsauthorpage/

And closest to my black heart is my reader fan group,

Holly's Hellions. Become a Hellion. Raise Hell. www.facebook.com/groups/hollyshellions/

Cheers!

Holly Roberds

WANT A FREE BOOK?

Join Holly's Newsletter Holly's Hot Spot at www. hollyroberds.com and get the Five Orders Prequel Novella, The Knight Watcher, for FREE!

Plus you'll get exclusive sneak peaks, giveaways, fun lil' nuggets, and notifications when new books come out. Woot!

ACKNOWLEDGMENTS

This book has been a long time coming. From the moment I put this antihero on the page in Prophecy Girl in 2017 - I knew his secret damage. This antihero pops up as frequently as Krystan and Travis because he has always been irresistible. The reluctant hero who can't even see all that he does.

Thank you Jolene Perry - you've been with me since the beginning and it's so gratifying to have an editor experience this full circle moment with me.

Thank you to Christie Hartman who cleans my books up until they shimmer and shine! Your eye is impeccable and I'm so grateful you let me skate in, even 3 weeks later than I say I will because I think we are aware that is who I am by now lol.

To my emotional support Canadian, Sarah Urquhart, yet again I worried about the spice and pondered pulling back only to watch you shift into a threatening Wolverine. Yet again, this book remains at the top spice rack level because of you.

To my Coffee & Characters writer group - Ellie Pond, CS Berry, Sarah Urquhart, Selena Blake, Daniela Romero, Ivy Nelson and more - my god, we are absolute chaos, and I love every moment of it. We support each other so hard core and there is no problem or question we cannot find the answer too. I feel like a powerhouse because of your support.

Leah Crowell - damn you were the best idea I ever had! Because of your AMAZING assistance, I have jumped leaps and bounds. You are worthy of the title, Hellfire Assistant!

To my family and friends, I have never lost sight of how you have always and continually support this path. I am keenly aware not everyone gets this kind of love and support and it makes my heart want to explode like gory confetti.

And thank you to l'husbun. You have always been a believer in me, and support me in all the ways from feeding me, calming me down, to making sure I celebrate every tiny little milestone. You are my real life romance and HEA.

ABOUT THE AUTHOR

Holly started out writing Buffy the Vampire Slayer and Terminator romantic fanfiction before spinning off into her own fantastic worlds with apocalyptic stakes.

Holly is a Colorado girl, but is only outdoorsy in that she likes drinking on patios in Denver.

She lives with her husband whose handsome looks are only out done by his charming and wicked supportive personality.

Surly house rabbits supervise this writer, to make sure she doesn't spend all of her time watching Buffy reruns.

For more sample chapters, news, and more, visit www.hollyroberds.com